Wanderer Among Shadows

Wanderer Among Shadows

Genavieve Blackwood

Dedicated to Irma and Darlene,
two of the strongest women I have ever had the honor of knowing.
And to Melissa Joan, who I hope has found peace.

"Melancholy and imagination hath fancied many things to proceed from witches, when there is no ground for it."

-John Hale, *A Modest Enquiry into the Nature of Witchcraft*

PROLOGUE

She stands in a courtroom filled with noisy spectators. Angry shouts and pointing fingers are directed at her. The clerk quickly records what is said, dipping his quill into the ink well every few seconds. She cannot see the faces of the magistrates in the dim candlelight, but they are there in their black clothing and she can feel them glaring at her. A neighbor appears in the crowd to make hasty accusations against her and she feels anger and betrayal well up inside of her. One of the magistrates asks her questions, but she has failed to prepare a proper defense and nonsensical answers fall from her lips. And so it follows that the court hands down the verdict and her grisly sentence.

The dream startles me from my restless slumber. My heart pounds incessantly and the anxiety fills me once again. I have had so many dreams similar to this one. They are distorted from the reality of the events, but they are nonetheless true. It has been ten years since those events and the nightmares still plague me. The memories still creep back into my mind. All the hatred, the sadness, the abuse come flooding back with a vengeance to drown me. Happiness is hard to find when you are lost in the wilderness of your own despair.

The trickle of children's laughter filters in through the open lattice-paned window. It pulls me back to the world of the living for a brief moment. A moment is all I am given before I find myself residing amongst the damned once again. Some mornings I find it hard to pull myself out of bed. This is one of those mornings. I walk over to the window and gaze out onto the scene below. The sun has already been overhead for many hours now. A light breeze dances across my skin despite the summer warmth pervading the air.

My children run about as they chase each other in some game of their own creation. Most parents would disapprove of such wild behavior, but I prefer to allow my children to revel in their youth before it is gone forever. A bittersweet smile comes to my lips. I would give anything to relive my own carefree days, but unfortunately, lost time cannot be regained. I will have to live vicariously through my children and, if I am lucky enough to still walk this earth, my grandchildren as well.

Footsteps echo in from the hall. I do not turn because I recognize the steady gait and know who the footsteps belong to. My husband walks softly over to me. A gentle hand finds its way to my shoulder and he kisses my cheek.

"How did you sleep?" His voice is soft.

"Restful," I reply with a tired smile as I turn to look at him.

He knows my answer is a lie. He knows all of my darkest thoughts and my most painful memories. He knows my mannerisms and the words I use to hide the truth from him. Despite his best attempts, my melancholy remains and it has affected him as well. But he has remained by my side, determined to reignite a light within my soul that has long since been extinguished.

"Sarah, you look not well rested at all," is his soft reply. "Tell me, was it another dream?"

I turn from him and nod. "I was back in the courtroom. There were so many people shouting at me and I found myself incapable of speech."

He sighs. "Love, I pray every day that there will come a time when the only dreams you have are of an endless summer day."

"What I would give for that," I murmur to myself.

Gently, he wraps his arms around me and I lean back into him, taking comfort in his embrace. He runs a hand over my growing belly. I am expecting our fourth child in five months' time. There were times when I feared I would not have this; that I would not be a mother or have a loving, caring husband. Now I have a girl and two boys, and I have a suspicion that the next will be a girl. And it is for his sake and for the sake of our family that I sluggishly get dressed and begin my daily chores. It is for their sake that I try to find little things to take comfort in and to smile about. The times that I feel genuinely happy and smile are few and the other times I pretend as a courtesy to those around me. My suffering has lessened over the years, but it is still present, always within me.

As I walk out into the yard, I feel the warmth of the sun upon my face. The fields are bursting with life and all is lush and green. There is always a certain wonder I feel in watching the plants begin life anew every year.

"Mama!" I hear a cheerful cry behind me. Turning, I see my eldest child, my eight-year-old daughter, Mary, running toward me. "The roses have started to bloom already."

"Have they now?" I smile down at her. "Well, I must go see."

I let her lead me to the garden where we always grow the roses. They are shades of bright red and pink and their colors stand out in the otherwise green expanse.

"They are so beautiful, and they are plentiful this year," she remarks. Indeed, the bush has grown back fuller this year than last. "Papa said you have always grown them," she says, turning toward me.

"Yes, since I was a girl," I reply. "My parents let me tend to them every year." She looks away from me and I can tell she is thinking of something. "What is on your mind, little one?"

"I… I hardly ever hear you talk about your own parents, especially your mama," she says timidly.

"It is because it makes me sad to speak of them, especially my mother," I reply, trying hard to swallow unshed tears. "I named you after her, you know?"

"Yes, I believe you have told me so before," she replies. "I should like to know more about her." She looks up at me shyly, but there is hope in her eyes.

I calm her fear of upsetting me with another smile. "Perhaps I will share some of my happier memories with you," I explain. "When you are older, when you can understand better, I will tell you the entire truth. But until then, take satisfaction with what I can relate."

Mary nods and returns my smile. I cannot remember much of what I looked like at her age, but she shares so many of my features that the likeness is uncanny. And with her sharp wit and love of the outdoors, no one could doubt she is my child. I look upon her tenderly and caress her cheek before kissing her forehead. I never knew I could love someone so much. It amazes me always.

I take her smaller hand in mine and we walk to where we grow the herbs. She helps me gather some to hang in the house for drying. She is already a little lady, but is still so young. She knows not of the world's cruelties yet, and I intend to keep her from them for as long as I can. But alas, there will come a day when I can shelter her no longer and my heart breaks at the thought. There will be a day when she, like everyone else, will lose her innocence and will have to be hardened against the harsh realities of the world. I can only hope that whatever burdens she may have to bear, they will never be near to what I have endured.

CHAPTER ONE

Ten years earlier – April 3, 1692
Andover, Massachusetts

"Wake up!"

The loud voice startled Sarah Parker out of her deep sleep. Her breathing and heartbeat became rapid in her shaken state and she turned to see her younger brother smirking at her.

"Christ almighty, Peter!" she growled. "What are you doing? The sun is not yet up!"

"I know, but we are already one year older." He smiled obnoxiously.

"Why did God have to curse me to share a date of birth with you?" she asked in exasperation. Oddly enough, the two youngest Parker children were indeed born on the same date, albeit six years apart.

"Because God loves me," he replied in a tone of mock pride. "I will leave you to finish resting now." He bowed his head to her before leaving her bedroom.

Sarah sighed. "He behaves worse than his nephews," she muttered. As her brother grew older, he became more wavering in his demeanor. One moment he could be cheerful and have endless energy, the next he would be sullen and brooding in a corner. Being that he was sixteen now, she hoped he would start acting like a man and not a boy.

She turned on her side and faced the window. The sun was beginning to rise, painting the sky in shades of orange and light blue. Sarah got out of bed and walked to the window. She could feel a slight draft coming from the sill. Early April still brought cold days and she could not wait for the warmth of summer. A surge of happiness ran through her as she pictured blooming roses and fluttering butterflies. She was always a child of the summer, never of the winter.

Turning back to her room, she had a keen sense of just how empty it had become. She had previously shared this room with her elder sisters, but they had since married and moved out. After her father's death seven years ago, the eldest sibling in the family, John, had married and their mother had given up her room to the couple. She stayed in Sarah's room for awhile, but as the younger sons in the family got bigger and John started having children of his own, it was decided that the spacious attic would make for a more comfortable sleeping area for the boys in the house. The two youngest brothers were tired of living in cramped quarters for so many years and welcomed the change. And so it was that Sarah's mother and brothers had been kind enough to allow Sarah to keep the room to herself while her mother took the boys' old bedroom. Sarah enjoyed her privacy in the always crowded house.

Yet, there was a nagging feeling within her. She turned twenty-two today and ever present in her mind was the expectation to find a husband soon. This expectation created a conflict within her. Of course she wanted a husband and children, but part of her didn't feel ready for marriage, fearing the changes it would bring in her life. If she felt she had little freedom and independence now, she would certainly have none as a wife and mother. But what other path was there for her in life?

Putting the thought aside, she proceeded to get dressed for the day. Carefully, she untangled her honey brown hair from her nightcap and brushed it free of knots. She had always taken pride in her long, soft locks, which her mother disapproved of as vanity. Yet, she could not help but feel it was her prettiest feature. Her hair though was in fierce competition with another one of her features—her eyes. Most people were instantly captivated by her bright blue eyes, especially as they often appeared near turquoise in color. Her father once remarked they could reflect a stormy sea one moment and a clear summer sky the next. She put on her good cream-colored dress that she normally wore for the Sabbath and pinned her hair up before putting on her day cap.

Sarah walked downstairs to the dining area. She was the first one to be prepared for the day, thanks to Peter. She took solace in the quiet of the room before the rest of the family got up. Her brother John came downstairs next with his four-year-old son, Jacob, bounding down the stairs next to him.

"Good morning," he greeted his sister. John too had blue eyes, but his were the shade of their mother's muted blue. He was a man of average height, barely taller than Sarah, but what he lacked in inheriting their father's imposing build, he made up for in his stern nature.

"Good morning," she replied just as her nephew ran straight to her. He grabbed onto her skirt and looked up at her with big, excited eyes.

"Papa says today marks the day of your birth," he said hurriedly, words coming out in a jumble.

"It does." She smiled down at him. "Your Uncle Peter's as well."

"Will we celebrate?" He waited expectantly.

"I fear not." What she truly wanted to say was that they would instead be punished by having to sit through the tedious Sabbath services, but thought better of it with the child's father in the room. "Although I suppose giving our due respect to God today is in a way celebrating."

"Oh," he groaned and turned away from her despondently. She tried in vain to stop herself from smirking at his blatant displeasure of having to sit through mass, a displeasure she shared.

Ann, John's wife, came downstairs next with their other son, eighteen-month-old Nathan, named for his deceased grandfather. She greeted Sarah brightly as she held her son close to her chest. Ann was a short woman who had grown plump after childbirth. She had a warm, inviting demeanor which was highlighted by her round, almost childlike face and the bouncy blonde curls that would sometimes peek out from beneath her cap. Sarah got along well with Ann, but she felt neither one way nor the other about her sister-in-law. She was kind enough, but Sarah found nothing interesting about her.

Perhaps, however, that was what made her so appealing to John. He had grown to be a ruthlessly practical man. Everything he did needed to have purpose grounded in reality, and a submissive, gentle wife who performed her duties and nothing more was exactly what he wanted. And it was this trait of his that caused him to clash often with his youngest sister. Sarah was headstrong and perhaps at times could be too much of a dreamer. Sometimes she would be found spending far too much time in the garden or staring up at the sky. It was not that she was lazy—in fact, she was very diligent in her chores—but she often found her mind wandering to things less mundane. It was as if she desired of a better world than the one in which she lived. John found no use for such musings.

Sarah found herself avoiding conversation with her oldest brother as much as possible, instead taking company with her other brother Joseph, who had just made his way into the dining room. They were very close as he was only one year older than her. He was taller than any of the other family members, and most of the people in Andover for that matter. He had a well-built frame and strong, handsome facial features. His thick, chocolate brown waves and golden hazel eyes, which he inherited from his father, made him a head turner in the community. He preferred to keep things light and simple, often jesting and taking nothing too seriously. Sarah found his personality to be much more agreeable than those of her other brothers.

Peter and their mother, Mary, were the last to come into the room. As Sarah observed her younger brother, he looked to be a shorter, thinner version of

Joseph, except that he shared Sarah's lighter brown hair. She wouldn't be surprised if he ended up being taller than Joseph, with his gangly limbs showing signs of more growth. Their mother smiled as she bade Sarah good morning. Mary was the vision of matronly perfection in their society. Now in her late fifties, she had spent most of her life giving her husband numerous children and raising them to be respectable adults. She knew when to speak and when to let her husband and sons take care of matters. She was a devout woman who was vigilant in her Christian duties. Still, she managed to be caring and understanding toward her children and mindful of their needs.

They sat to eat their morning meal, which they had prepared the day before. Light conversation was made and in the midst of it Sarah brought up how her brother rudely awakened her.

"Peter, enough of this childishness," her mother scolded him. "Let your sister alone."

"Why? She is not the one getting kicked and pushed all night long." He pouted as he turned to look at Joseph.

"I cannot help it if my legs are too long," Joseph defended himself.

"Make a separate cot for yourself then if it bothers you that much," Sarah curtly told Peter. She was tired of hearing about his nighttime complaints and wished he would do something about it. Like a petulant child, he scrunched up his nose and growled at her in response.

"Peter, please," came the exasperated sigh from their mother.

Joseph giggled to himself and playfully said to

Peter, "You best pray for forgiveness today or I may have to beat good behavior into you."

"You do that enough already," Peter shot back at him. "And I have the bruises on my legs to prove it."

Sarah shook her head, visualizing how the rest of the family felt. After their meal was finished, they set out for mass. Sarah wrapped her cloak tightly around her as the chilly April air hit her. Her nephew soon began to whine about the cold and long walk and eventually John picked him up to make him stop. Upon arriving at the meetinghouse, they met their sister Hannah and her husband, Daniel Tyler, and their three boys and baby daughter. Hannah was in her early thirties and the Parkers' eldest surviving daughter after the passing of their sister, also named Mary. Despite having four children, Hannah managed to remain stick thin, which was only emphasized by her height. She shared Joseph's shade of hair and eye color and she likewise was tall like him. There was no mistaking that they were siblings.

Hannah was usually quiet in public, preferring to keep out of local gossip, and was careful about how she presented herself when in the company of others. She wasn't always like this, but that was before she had brought scandal to the family. Shortly after her marriage, her husband admitted to fornicating with her before they were wed and the two were brought to court for it. Her parents had been disappointed, but they largely blamed her behavior on her husband. The Tylers weren't without scandal themselves and behind closed doors, Hannah's parents found Daniel to be the one who led her astray. Hannah had defended him, of course, claiming that she was equally to blame. Although her family had forgiven her, the embarrassment caused her to be more withdrawn and strait-laced as an attempt to show the community that she had repented for her past transgression.

Sarah went to the pew the female members of her family normally sat in. Her friend Lydia Holten was already there waiting for her. She was a few years younger than Sarah, but Sarah enjoyed her company. Lydia had a vibrant personality that always managed to make Sarah feel better no matter how bad her mood was.

"Good morning, Sarah. If I remember correctly today marks your twenty-second year." Lydia greeted her with a pleasant smile, and her gray eyes sparkled.

"Good morning, and yes, it does." Sarah returned her smile.

"And that would mean that Peter is older as well?" she asked.

"Yes, but still regressing in maturity."

Lydia laughed at that, having heard far too much about him from Sarah. She tucked a piece of auburn hair back under her cap and slyly used it to disguise that her eyes were wandering around the meetinghouse. She let them fall on one particular gentleman. "Samuel Galler keeps looking this way, you know," she said quietly as she leaned into Sarah. "I believe he has his eye on you. In fact, I noticed his eyes have not left you since you walked in."

Slowly, Sarah looked out of the corner of her eye in Samuel's direction, and sure enough the young man was looking at her. When he saw that she had noticed, he turned around quickly in an awkward fashion.

"Yes, he has been doing that for the past several

weeks," Sarah muttered, trying to hide the smile that played on her lips.

"And you have done naught about it?" Lydia's jaw nearly dropped at her friend's lack of action.

"What is there to do besides to tell him to keep his eyes to himself?" Sarah was only being half serious, of course. She didn't particularly dislike his attention, but she was too unsure of how she felt about him in that regard to even consider talking to him about it. She knew him well enough from when he would sometimes come to the Parker household to exchange goods or crops with them from his own home. He seemed kind enough, but how would he be as a husband?

Lydia continued, sounding as if she were trying to persuade her on his behalf. "Well, he comes from a respectable family... and he is quite handsome."

"You lead me to believe you want him for yourself." A touch of jealousy laced Sarah's words.

"Oh no, I just want to see you round with child so that I can finally say you are bigger than me." She began to giggle at her own teasing remarks.

"Oh you little... You are terrible!" Sarah playfully slapped her friend's arm and laughed herself.

She heard her mother clear her throat and the two fell silent, trying to stop themselves from laughing further. Sarah slowly turned to look at her mother, who had an eyebrow raised at her. Heat rose in her face from embarrassment and she cast her eyes downward. As she sat waiting for the service to begin, her thoughts wandered back to Samuel. She might not have admitted it out loud, but Sarah did agree with Lydia that he was handsome with his jet black hair and icy blue eyes. Even if she considered him as a potential spouse one day, she feared that her family may not approve of the match. While his family was well off, the Gallers had less wealth and property than her own and her family probably would think she could do better.

"Mother, Sarah." Hearing a voice behind them, Sarah and Mary turned to see Elizabeth, the middle sister of the Parker family, and her young daughter rushing into their seats behind them. Elizabeth looked flushed and was out of breath. In contrast to Joseph, Elizabeth was the shortest member of the family. She looked a lot like Sarah, but had more of their father's facial features.

"Elizabeth? Are you well?" Mary asked in concern.

"Yes, James was being so fussy this morning," she replied, referring to her baby son. "And this one nearly burnt the house down." She looked crossly at the little girl beside her who turned her face away in shame.

"What happened?" Sarah inquired.

"She knocked one of the candles over this morning and set a piece of parchment on fire," she answered with a sigh. "Thankfully Henry has quick hands and put it out." Henry, her husband, was a member of the Farnum family.

"I did not mean it. It was but an accident," her daughter said quietly.

Elizabeth sighed and then said more softly, "I know, my dear, but you must be more careful." Elizabeth had inherited their mother's warmth.

The last of the parishioners filtered into the meetinghouse and took their seats. A hush fell over the building as Reverend Thomas Barnard, the younger of the town's two ministers, walked up to the pulpit to begin the service. Like all services, this one ambled on as usual, only being broken up by a psalm or some noisy children becoming restless. Sarah felt herself dozing off a few times, finding that staying alert was made harder as a result of Peter waking her up too early. Finally, Reverend Barnard came to his lengthy sermon regarding one of the passages from the Bible that he had read.

"Remember, God hath granted you life and it is by His will that he suffers you to live in his creation despite your flaws. To forget that He is your true master would be to condemn yourselves." His voice became more severe at this point in the sermon and commanded attention throughout the meetinghouse. "Let not the weaknesses within yourselves tempt you to the devil's hand. Do not seek out practices which would circumvent providence to fulfill your earthly desires and would in so doing corrupt your souls."

This part of his sermon was no doubt alluding to the recent chaos that had taken hold in Salem Village. Tales of afflicted children being harassed by servants of the devil were enough to scare many of the God-fearing people of Massachusetts. It stirred up anxiety about who among them just may be a witch in hiding. Sarah just hoped that any witches would remain in Salem.

When mass finally ended, everyone began to make their way out of the meetinghouse. Sarah saw Samuel not far behind her. She wasn't sure what to say to him, but she purposely slowed down. She soon felt him fall into step beside her. "So, have you been meaning to tell me something? Or perhaps you find my face not to your liking?" she finally asked, turning to him. She was surprised at how tall he was, nearly as tall as Joseph.

His cheeks colored at her questions, but he retained his composure. "Forgive me. I did not mean to stare," he said, then a bit more boldly, "And if I do, it is only because I find your face to be much to my liking."

It was her turn to blush at his forwardness and for a moment she found herself speechless before asking, "So you are confident enough to stare at me, but not speak to me?" She was trying to press him for more information about how he felt about her.

"I am speaking to you now, am I not?" he asked in return.

She sighed. "Samuel, in all the time I have known you, you have never once spoken to me beyond common pleasantries. Tell me truthfully then, what do you want of me now?"

"I like to think myself not so dull as to be unable to converse in more thoughtful matters. Would you and I not make agreeable company in that regard? Or perhaps her highness thinks me beneath her?" He smirked at her as he spoke the last sentence.

She could tell by the look in his eyes, however, that he was trying to hide his nervousness behind a false bravado. "If you are merely trying to relate that you would like to know me better then make it plain."

"Very well then," he breathed out deeply, "I have come to realize of late that I have been a fool not to have taken more notice of your pleasant face and wish to know you better."

She was sure she had turned a fierce shade of scarlet by now. "And it would seem you have more than friendship in mind," she stated quietly as she turned to look at him. There was an awkward silence between them for a brief moment as they stared at each other.

"Amazing," he whispered as he looked into her eyes. "I have never seen anyone with blue eyes of that shade."

"Most people have not." She looked into his eyes as well, trying to search for his true self in them.

His face turned more serious under the scrutiny of her gaze. "I wish you would not look at me like that. I feel as if you are trying to lay bare my very soul." It both unnerved and fascinated him just how expressive and soulful her eyes seemed.

"Sarah!" Before she could respond, Joseph's call broke the couple's attention toward one another. "Will you hurry up? Or do I have to scare the young man away from you?" He mischievously grinned at the two, knowing full well what was passing between them.

"Afraid she likes talking to me more than you?" Samuel jokingly replied.

"Only in your dreams, Galler! No one makes for better conversation than I!" he called back as he walked on with the rest of the family.

They came to the spot in the road where their paths differed. "I shall speak to you again then?" Samuel asked her with light timidity. Sarah could not help but find it endearing.

"I would like that." She gave him a small smile before bidding him good day and continuing on the path to her house.

༄

That night the moon was full and bright, illuminating the sky. Sarah stood by her bedroom window gazing out at the celestial body. She had always found the moon to be a calming sight as it serenely sat in the heavens.

"I often wonder if you wait for the moon to speak to you." Her mother's amused voice came from outside her bedroom door.

She turned to give her mother a soft smile. "In its own way, it already does," she said, turning back to the moon.

"And what doth it say?" Mary joined her at the window.

"Fear not, for I will guide thy way in the dark," she said, then turned back to Mary. "Or so I imagine that is what it would say." She gave another small smile and her mother smiled back.

"This is the most I have seen you smile in a single day in a long time," Mary said. "'Tis no wonder though, given Samuel Galler's attention towards you today." There it was. Sarah knew she would be unable to avoid this conversation.

"Plain conversation was all it was." Her tone became too defensive too quickly.

"So it was only the cold reddening your cheeks then?" Mary continued to prod.

"Mother, please!" Sarah was sure she was blushing again and wished her mother would turn to any other conversation.

"Sarah you are more than old enough to marry now, you must not shy away from speaking of possible matches," Mary stated. "How do you feel about him anyway?"

Sarah sighed, giving into her mother's talk of

matchmaking. "I cannot say," she replied. "He appears kind, but I know not of the man well enough to judge how he would be as a husband."

Her mother, of course, thought more in practical terms than in matters of the heart. "He comes from a respectable family… but perhaps you could find a man of better means."

"I care not so much for that as I do about where his heart lies," Sarah explained. "I want a husband who will be mindful of my intellect and not simply relegate me to the caretaking of children; one who will understand the things I enjoy and not take them from me."

"I understand. Perhaps you will be fortunate enough to find such a husband." Mary gently laid a hand on her daughter's head. "But be patient; it often takes time for men to show such attributes." She had had similar fears upon her marriage to Nathan, especially as her husband had been more than a decade older than her. At the start of their marriage she sometimes felt he treated her as a child, but as she matured, he regarded her as more his equal. The two had grown more akin to best friends than husband and wife as the years wore on and she was grateful for it.

"I can only hope," Sarah said quietly to herself.

"Oh, I nearly forgot." Mary suddenly exited the room as she remembered something, confusing Sarah. When she returned she had a pair of small embroidery scissors in her hand. "For your birthday. I know you have been in need of a new pair."

It was a small gesture, but it meant so much to Sarah as most people did nothing to commemorate their birthdays. Her mother always found little ways

21

to do something special for her children. "Thank you, Mother, truly." She smiled.

Mary smiled back and kissed her forehead. "Goodnight, my dearest."

"Goodnight, Mother," she returned. And with a warmth in her chest that had been missing all winter long, Sarah went to sleep.

CHAPTER TWO

Chilly April eventually turned to May and with it came warmer days. The family, like most others, became more preoccupied with the planting and growing of their crops. It was exhausting, but necessary work. Sarah was probably the only member of the family who genuinely found any joy in it. Late spring and summer gave her more opportunities to get out of the stuffy house and she would certainly take them. She also always took pride in watching the plants she had worked hard tending grow to full bloom and bear fruit.

On a breezy but warm day, while the men were busy working in the fields, Sarah found herself tending to the seedlings in the herb garden. They grew many herbs such as parsley, rosemary, and dill. Most of them were for medicinal or culinary purposes, but Sarah sometimes liked to gather a few to keep in her bedroom for their scent. She was no stranger to going up and down the rows of herbs to rub their leaves and inhale the lovely fragrances they created.

Sarah took her time tending to the garden. She would stop every now and then to stretch her back and look at the sky. It was clear blue today with only a few puffy clouds. Sunlight illuminated the clouds, giving them an ethereal glow. Sometimes she wondered what it would be like to lie on a cloud, just slowly drifting through the sky. Would it be like sleeping on a bed, only softer? Or maybe it would be like getting caught in the wispy threads of a spider's web after the fluffier parts of the cloud dispersed under your weight. Before she became too lost in her own imagination, she turned back to her work and gave her attention to the seedlings once again.

"May I help?" a tiny voice beside her asked.

She jumped, startled at not having heard anyone approach. She turned to see Jacob at her side. "You startled me," she breathed.

"Sorry," he muttered.

"It is all right, and yes, you may help," she replied. She showed him how to tend to the soil and pull out newly grown weeds without disturbing the seedlings. As he was working, he bent over to pull out a weed and tripped on his skirt. Thankfully, he was quick to react and stopped himself from hitting his face on the ground. As children often do at that age, he quickly got back up and brushed off his hands.

"Are you hurt?" Sarah asked, going over to him.

"No, but this would be easier were I not in a skirt," he said. "When shall I have breeches like Papa?"

"Usually not for a few more years," she replied. "But perhaps if you can show what a hardworking little man you have become, you will have them sooner than that."

"Then I shall certainly work hard." He smiled at her before going to work more vigorously in the garden.

She smiled to herself at his determination, but also as she thought of the day when she would have her own children to raise. She had proven to be good at taking care of her nieces and nephews and everyone always commented on how she would make an excellent mother. Sometimes Jacob would come to her instead of his mother for company or to sit on her lap. Although Ann never said anything, Sarah wondered if it bothered her. She never meant to usurp the mother's place, but she enjoyed being with the little ones and knew the experience would help her in the future.

When their work was finished, she led Jacob back inside. "Thank you for letting me help!" He beamed at her. He was always eager to work and learn new things.

After a long day of tilling and planting in the yard, the family sat around the hearth as night descended. Mary was sitting in the corner, sewing something by candlelight. Sarah sat quietly by her side, looking at her mother's work. When Sarah inquired as to what it was she was sewing, Mary only dismissed it as another apron she was sewing for herself. Sarah couldn't help but notice her mother's aprons were in nearly pristine condition, but she didn't question her as to why she needed another one. Instead, she turned her attention to her nephew, who was standing next to his father watching him carving wood. John explained the process to his son and the little boy was transfixed on every word and movement of his hands. Most importantly, Sarah saw the affection in John's eyes when he looked at his son and the tenderness in his voice when he spoke to the boy. She wished her brother showed this warmth and calmness more often than he did. Rarely did he partake in leisure activities such as this.

Looking at John teaching his son and reflecting on what she taught her nephew today, it made her think of her father. Sarah missed her father deeply and most importantly the times like this that they would share together. Nathan knew from an early age that Sarah was an intelligent child with a deep desire for learning new things and he took joy in teaching her all that he could. She was a quick student too and always wanted to do her part in the household. He never treated her like a child, but always like a young adult. Sadly, her father was already nearly fifty by the time she was born and it was inevitable that her time with him would be short. She just wished that she had been older when God had taken him home so that she would have been more mature and therefore would have appreciated him better.

There was much she wished for. She wished her siblings Mary, Robert, and James were still alive. While she had been closer with some siblings more than others, she wanted the family to be whole again. She wanted to see them all in their old age laughing and griping about their troublesome grandchildren and their aches and pains. Stopping herself, she shook the thoughts from her head, not wanting to drag her spirits down by thinking of past losses or regrets. She was alive and she still had her whole life ahead of her. She must think of the future and the good things that awaited her.

One of those things, of course, was a certain young man who gave her reason to be joyous this spring. It had become habitual every Sunday that she took some time when the chance arose to speak to Samuel. Getting to know him better with each passing week, she felt her heart growing fonder of the young man. As they grew more comfortable with each other, she found him easy to talk to. She found out more about him as well. He was a year older than Sarah and he and his younger brother George were the only living sons of his parents, the rest having died when they were young children. He also once had dreams of living a life at sea, but as he grew older he realized there were too many dangers that came with seafaring and that he was needed at home with his family. Sarah even found that they shared taking pleasure in many of the same things such as stargazing and taking care of the family horses. Slowly, she was starting to see him as a man she could marry. Still, she wanted to know how he would act as a husband toward her. She didn't want to ask him outright or unburden all her fears to him at this early stage. She just needed a subtle way to gauge his character better.

One Sunday, she received her chance. It was early May and the weather was nice enough that some people decided to wait outside the meetinghouse before services started. They spent time conversing with each other, catching up on the latest gossip. Before going inside to sit in their respective seats, Sarah and Samuel were talking when they spotted Elizabeth and her husband arguing about something or other. Their fight caught the attention of some people nearby who stopped mid-conversation to look at them.

Her husband managed to silence her by saying rather violently, "Woman, do as I bid you! I will hear no more of this!"

Elizabeth looked angry and her cheeks reddened in embarrassment. He walked on ahead of her and she went to tend to her children, trying to act as if nothing happened. It was not the first time that Sarah had seen them arguing in such a fashion and it made her angry. While she did not doubt her brother-in-law loved her sister, he certainly did not like having his authority questioned, especially by his wife. Using her sister's situation, she took the opportunity to pry an answer to her concerns from Samuel.

"I pray to God I never marry such a man," she spoke quietly, but just loud enough for him to hear her.

"I have never understood men who give no respect to the women who bear their children," he returned, looking absently at her sister.

She turned to look at him and could not help but smile, for he had passed her test. *Yes*, she thought, *this is a man worthy of my hand.*

He faced her once again and became confused upon seeing her smile. "What is it?" he asked and a smile that stretched to his eyes came upon his face as well.

He had a beautiful smile indeed and whenever he smiled at her, she could not help but lose her composure. "Nothing," she replied and her smile only deepened at his.

Eventually, they had to cease their conversation and go inside. Every so often though throughout the mass, they would look in the other's direction and catch their eye. They would give each other a little knowing grin. He shared her dislike of sitting through the lengthy Sabbath service as well.

What Sarah did not know was that her mother observed these encounters with a careful eye. Not only was she watchful for any signs of possible indecent conduct after what happened with Hannah, but she was looking for signs of her daughter's inner feelings about Samuel. After sometime, Mary began to recognize the look in her daughter's eyes, having had it in her own and having seen it with her other children often enough. Even if Sarah did not know it herself yet, Mary knew that there would be no convincing her daughter to marry another now. And with how stubborn her daughter could be at times, Mary had to resign herself to the fact. As long as Samuel could provide for Sarah and make her happy, then that would just have to be enough for Mary. *After all, he may grow to have better standing as the years pass,* she thought. Her own husband had started off as nothing more than an indentured servant, but he managed to grow his wealth and property over the years.

Mary did not let her thoughts continue beyond that, as she tried to avoid thinking of her late husband Nathan as much as possible. Thinking of him made her sad and she longed to be with him again. There were nights when she would be alone in her room and cry looking at the empty side of the bed, wishing he was still at her side. While he had been there to see Hannah and Elizabeth wed, she wished he could have been there when John married and when hopefully the rest of their children would. She wanted him to see their grandchildren grow. But alas, it was not to be. She took comfort in the possibility that perhaps his spirit would come to them every so often and that he could see their expanding family.

She tried to focus instead on the family still with her. In particular, she enjoyed seeing her grandchildren grow and loved having little ones around the house again. She may even have more soon if Sarah married, and she finally thought that perhaps this match with Samuel was for the best. Mary sometimes worried about Sarah, who often seemed to travel to a world of fantasy in her mind, imagining things beyond her reach. Marrying may ground her by giving her a purpose and having children would be a necessary distraction. She could only hope for her daughter's welfare in the future.

cs

As the middle of May approached, temperatures rose and brought balmy weather with them. There was an ease among the parishioners as they met for Sunday service. They found the meetinghouse comfortable to be in for the time being, but it would become unbearably hot once summer fully hit. For once, Sarah didn't feel restless sitting through mass and actually felt content with her life at the moment. Her family members were all healthy and thriving, she and Samuel were growing closer, and summer would soon be here. She had nothing to complain of.

The service seemed to mirror her state of mind. It was much more uplifting than the others had been of late. When a psalm began, the voices that rang out in the room all seemed to be cheerful. In the middle of it though, another voice broke the harmonious sound made by the others. A few pews ahead of her, Sarah could see a girl acting as if she were trying to shake someone off of her. She kept shrugging her shoulder forward as if someone were holding onto it. Looking a little harder, she could see it was Phoebe Chandler. Listening as hard as she could, Sarah was just able to make out what the girl said against the singing.

"I will not tell you," Phoebe hissed out. "Let me alone, Goody Carrier."

Sarah was suddenly filled with great foreboding and something akin to disappointment knowing what would come from the girl's words. For unless her eyes were deceiving her, Goody Carrier was nowhere near the Chandler girl.

CHAPTER THREE

By the end of May, news of Martha Carrier's arrest was spreading around Andover. Some, like Mary, feared this would lead to an onslaught of witchcraft accusations against others in the town. Her sons were outside tending to the cornfields, making sure the soil was properly kept and the early corn shoots were growing right. She joined them and discussed the latest news as they worked.

"No surprise to me," Joseph remarked. "It is not the first time she has been accused of witchcraft."

"She should have been hanged two years ago when she killed half of her family," Peter added bitterly.

"'Twas smallpox that took them," John stated disapprovingly.

"Aye, and she brought it upon them," Peter shot back.

"You do not know that for certain," Mary reprimanded him. She found herself wary of these accusations. The sheer volume alone was off-putting and she wondered how so many people could have fallen into the devil's hand. Satan may very well have been deluding the accusers and she would not have her son believing their accusations so readily.

"But you must admit, there must be some substance behind the accusations for her to be brought up twice on this account," Joseph stated.

"And better to have her safely in prison than causing harm," Peter chimed in.

"Enough of that," Mary scolded. "Back to work with you two." The brothers exchanged glances before resuming their labor. Mary turned to John, who seemed to mirror his mother's own wariness.

"Fear not," he said soothingly. "I am sure the court will settle the matter and get to the truth of it."

As they continued conversing, they were unaware that they were being spied upon by a small figure. Upon hearing his family members talk of witches, Jacob became frightened and ran inside to his mother. Ann was helping Sarah in preparing the evening meal when her son ran up to her. He clutched at her skirt and tried to hide between her and his aunt.

"Jacob, what are you doing?" She was startled at his seemingly unprovoked behavior. "What happened?"

"The witches," he breathed. "I do not want them to hurt me."

"Witches? There are no witches here," she stated while prying his hands from her skirt.

"But Goody Carry is a witch!" He repeated what his family members discussed.

"You mean Goody Carrier?" Ann asked, hearing the mispronunciation, and Jacob nodded. She took his hands into her own and tried to explain the truth to him, "No, she was only accused. 'Tis not for certain if she is a witch. Either way, she is not here to harm you."

"But what if there are more witches?" He looked up at her with terrified eyes.

"Why do you come to believe there are witches here?" She waited for an answer, but when he did not give one, she continued, "Are not the people you know good persons?" He nodded then. "Then why would you believe any of them are witches out to hurt you?"

He shrugged his shoulders, unable to answer her question. Ann looked up at Sarah, hoping for help in calming her son. In truth, however, Sarah was uncertain of how she felt about the accusations. Were there really witches plaguing the county? Were the accusers so lost in their feverish fits that they knew not what they saw? Or far scarier, was the devil causing the entire ordeal to harm the innocent? She did not want to dwell on the situation, but she also did not want to frighten her nephew further.

"We would not let any harm come to you anyway," she finally stated. "We would protect you, would we not?" She looked at Ann, who nodded her assent.

"We would." Ann gently cupped her son's face in her hands. "Place your faith in us and in God that no witch will harm you."

He nodded and hugged his mother's legs, burying his face in her skirts. Ann sighed and stroked his hair to soothe him. When he finally calmed down, she set him to work helping in the kitchen. Quietly, she thanked Sarah for her help with him and her other son today. Nathan had been particularly restless and he only relaxed after Sarah had taken him into her arms. Her sister-in-law seemed to have an uncanny way of knowing just how to take care of children and rectifying their behavior in a subtle way. Sometimes Ann thought she wouldn't know what to do without her.

⚃

If there was one reason that Sarah liked the summer it was the dance of the fireflies. It was something she looked forward to every summer. She felt as if she could just sit for hours watching the dazzling show of lights in the darkness with not a sound but the chirping of crickets. Watching the whimsical routine of these insects always soothed her in both body and soul. Now she finally decided it was time to share the tradition with her nephew and figured that it would be a good way to distract him from the witches he seemed to fear so much.

"I believe it is finally warm enough for the fireflies to come out," she said to Jacob one night in June as she walked over to the window. Her nephew, curiosity piqued, came to her side and the two looked out the window as dusk fell. It was just about the right time of year to start seeing fireflies dancing about in the yard. Mary and Ann, who had been sitting nearby, shared knowing smiles with each other as they watched the two. Even if Mary sometimes worried about her daughter's childlike heart, she knew it would make the young woman's own children adore her in the future.

"Just wait and keep looking," Sarah said to Jacob as they waited expectantly by the window. Soon enough, yellow lights started to blink around the yard.

"Can we go out and see them?" he asked, turning to look at his mother.

"I suppose so." Ann smiled at him. "But not for too long, you must be in bed soon."

He nodded and then looked back to his aunt, who held out her hand to him. "Come," Sarah said just as eagerly as the boy was with taking her hand.

They walked out far enough away from the lights of the house so that they could see more fireflies passing by. Upon seeing some of the flickering lights, Jacob let his hand drop out of hers. He was about to run out further when Sarah stopped him with a hand on his shoulder. "You must wait till you see one light up, then follow its path," she explained.

They spotted one near to them and quickly followed it. Sarah could just barely make out the bug in the darkness and she caught it in her hands. Stooping down to her nephew's level, she opened her hand to reveal the bug to him. The firefly began to travel around her hand and crawled onto her finger.

"Can I hold it?" He held out his hands to her.

She carefully transferred it to her nephew's hand, having to pluck it off of her own. "Careful not to crush it," she said.

He nodded and followed the crawling insect's movements on his hand. The firefly then spread its wings and flew off into the night.

"Aw, he left." Jacob's face turned to dejection.

"Worry not, there are plenty more to catch." She waved her hand across the rest of the yard. Following her instructions, he sought out another one. Hearing footsteps behind her, she turned to see the boy's father coming over to them.

"Letting him chase after bugs now, are you?" John asked sternly.

"There is no harm in it." She shrugged her shoulders.

"He should be in bed at this hour." He shook his head.

"It only just turned dark," she replied. "Let him have some enjoyment for a time."

He sighed but said no more. Apparently his sister was now trying to impart this activity she had enjoyed in her own youth upon his son. Soon the toddler ran up to them, hands closed together. He thrust his hands up to his father, opening them only slightly. "Look! I caught one, Papa!" he exclaimed.

"Yes, so it seems." For a moment John's features softened at seeing his son's excitement. He decided that perhaps Sarah was right and so he let his son play out in the yard for a little longer. For once, he and his sister stood side by side, just taking in the little display that nature had gifted them and listening to the wonderful sound that was the laugh of a child.

 og

June would prove to be an eventful month. News of an attack by the French and their Native American allies on the English garrisons in Maine reached Andover by the middle of the month. Closer to home, the first person was hanged for witchcraft that year. Any hope that Mary and John had of the court dealing with the accusations fairly significantly diminished. The two sat by the hearth speaking quietly of the recent state of affairs.

"I fear constantly that trouble may fall upon us,"

Mary stated. "I fear that we may be raided by Indians or, God forbid, now with these witchcraft accusations…"

"Please do not worry yourself," John stated. "I do not think the Indians or the French would come this far south, and as for these accusations, those girls would hardly know any of the people in this town. Carrier was probably only named because of her previous infamy."

"Still, how are we to be assured of our safety? I heard Elizabeth Ballard is taken with illness similar to what the girls in Salem suffered," Mary explained. "What if she comes to believe it is the work of witches?"

"Well, it would certainly give her husband's brother more work." John referred to the town's constable, who was Elizabeth Ballard's brother-in-law.

"John, this is no time for jests." She stood up and began to pace back and forth. "What if she starts to name people?"

"Hopefully her illness can be remedied before it comes to that," he replied. "And if it is not, perhaps Reverend Dane can warn her away from accusing anyone." Dane was Andover's elder minister and had served the community for decades.

"Do you think Mr. Barnard will plead for caution?" she asked. "His fervor for condemning those who practice witchcraft hath been evident in his recent sermons."

"What he preaches and what he thinks may be two different things," John stated as he took a sip of his cider. "He may be more careful about finding out who actually is a witch first before he condemns them."

"I hope so. I do not want anyone of authority harming the innocent for the sake of righteous zeal," Mary sighed.

"I would like the same caution from the magistrates," John continued. "From what I hear, many of them are quite zealous in their pursuit to purge witches from the county."

"I want to trust in their abilities to discern who is a witch and who is not, but I have my doubts," Mary admitted.

"As do I. I would like to sit in on one of these proceedings to see if the evidence is really all that convincing." He got up then to stand in front of the fire.

"I do not doubt that there are witches among us or that certain persons perform devilish arts, but doth it not seem strange to you that so many have been accused?" she asked.

"I do not know many of those accused, but it seems suspicious to me that so many witches could be hiding among us and they only now choose to do evil." He gazed into the flames, as if searching them for answers. "And why would they make their persons known to the afflicted? People with malicious intentions do not seem the sort to readily condemn themselves."

"And why would they all choose to harm the same group of people? Would they not choose to harm others who have crossed them in some way?" Her mind was suddenly racing with questions.

"Mother, I believe we will drive ourselves to madness trying to understand this predicament." He turned to her in sympathy.

"I know, but there is so much that worries me of late. I grow weary of feeling this constant tension," she said as her throat became tight.

"Why do you feel it thus?" John inquired. "You cannot fear things which have not yet come to pass and which may never do so."

"I do not know," she answered honestly. "But every day this worry seizes upon my mind and I think of the worst that may happen this day or the next."

"Think not of it," he counseled, resting his hand on her shoulder comfortingly. "Whatever may come we will deal with accordingly. Until then, rest your mind."

CHAPTER FOUR

It was nearing the middle of July when Samuel came to visit the Parkers. Mary had inquired of his mother about yellow and red embroidery threads at mass and he insisted that he bring them over to her the next day. He went with a heavy heart, for he had information he needed to share with Sarah. He was sure she would not want to hear it, but he needed to relate it nonetheless. Joseph was the first person he saw as he approached the house.

"Samuel, good morning." Joseph stopped his work to greet him. "What brings you?"

"Good morning." He held up the embroidery threads. "Your mother requested these of my own."

"Ah yes, she said she would be needing them," he replied. "She is inside."

"Thank you." Samuel nodded at him before continuing onto the house. The door was open, but he stopped at the threshold before entering. Looking around, he saw Mary sweeping the floor. "Goody Parker," he called.

"Oh, hello, Samuel," she said as she looked up. "How are you today?"

"Fine, I suppose." He handed her the threads. "From my mother."

"Yes, give her my most sincere thanks." She smiled, but then frowned seeing his worried features. "Is something the matter?"

He hesitated for a moment before saying, "I fear I do not come under pleasant circumstances."

She listened attentively to what he had to say, knowing the distress this turn of events would bring not only him and his own family but her daughter as well. "Sarah is working outside, around back," she said, and then gently squeezed his arm. "God be with you."

He nodded solemnly. "Thank you."

He found Sarah crouched beside the carrot plants. She was presently preoccupied with checking to see how they were growing and removing those ready for harvest. She was sweating profusely in the heat and kept wiping her forehead off. Her basket was halfway filled with fresh carrots when her harvesting was interrupted by footsteps approaching. Turning, she saw Samuel approaching her and her expression immediately brightened upon seeing him.

"Sam!" she exclaimed, using the nickname he had told her to use.

"Sarah." He held out his hand to help her to her feet.

"Good to see you here," she said but then she noticed his downtrodden face. "Are you all right?"

"I must speak with you," he said softly.

"Very well, but let us go in the shade. The sun is brutal today." She led them to the back of the house,

44

which was partially covered in shade.

He stopped for a moment looking at the herb garden. A few vibrant winged butterflies flew in and out of the plants. In the corner was a large rose bush that was blossoming in a deep shade of pink. He reached out and gently touched one of the petals. "These are beautiful." He gave her a small smile. "Did you plant them yourself?"

"No, actually; they just started growing several years ago," she explained. "I know not how they came to be here, though I imagine it was the work of an animal burying seeds. I begged my parents to not rip them out and I have been tending to them ever since."

"You do a magnificent job," he complimented.

"Thank you, but please tell me what you wished to relate." She walked into the shade and removed her sun hat to look at him better.

He paused and sighed before finally telling her, "I am to go to Maine with the militia."

Upon hearing his words, she felt her heart crumble. "You have been pressed into service?" she asked frantically.

"They approached my brother first about serving, but I asked to go in his place." He cast his eyes down.

"Why would you do that? Did you have family who perished in the raids?" she questioned in disbelief.

"No, I did not, but I wish not to leave those still there unprotected," he spoke quietly. "As for why else I choose to go, I fear you may not understand my reasoning." How could he possibly explain to her the restlessness that had filled his soul these past several months? He needed change in his life; he needed to experience something beyond the endless cycle of farming and harvesting and going to mass.

"Then make me understand," she commanded. Her eyes were afire and his resolve weakened under her gaze.

"Why must you look at me like that?" He shook his head. "It is hard for me to explain. I just feel as if I will go mad if I have to stay here another year staring at the same crops, doing the same mindless tasks. I need something more in my life, another purpose."

"And how will you achieve that purpose if you are killed?" she snapped at him.

"The governor has been charged with rebuilding the fort at Pemaquid." He gave her more details concerning his service. "It is unlikely I will even see combat."

"But what if you are ambushed?"

"Then may God see to it that we are quick to react and defend ourselves."

There was silence between them for a long moment before she finally spoke. "You once told me that you realized your place was here, and now you are saying that this is no longer enough for you. Do you mean to abandon your family?" Then she asked even more quietly, "Abandon me?"

"Sarah, I am not abandoning anyone. I will return," he tried to reassure her and took her hand in his. "Honestly, you were one of the only reasons I had any hope of late. Without you, I may have left sooner. Please do not be angry with me." Of course, what he did not tell her was that she was actually one of the reasons he wanted to go. With the pay he would receive he could buy more land or look to other economic ventures. It could give him better standing and make him a better suited husband for her.

"I wish you would not go. I have already lost a brother in battle, I wish not to lose you as well." She looked down at their joined hands.

He gently pushed her chin up so that she was looking at him again. "I will come back to you," he stated firmly.

"You better, or I will give your spirit no rest." They gave each other pained smiles. "I will pray for you every night and every day."

"I shall take comfort in that." He squeezed her hand. "Until next time."

"Be safe." He nodded at her before turning away. She could have sworn there were tears at the edges of his eyes; there were certainly tears in her own. She stood motionless for a time, watching as he faded into the distance.

For the rest of the day, Sarah was quiet and withdrawn. As the sunset, she found herself sitting in solitude beneath the great oak tree in their yard. Normally, the shades of purple, red, and orange in the evening sky would be a welcome sight for her, but tonight they brought her no relief. The worry that filled her mind would not cease no matter how hard she tried to quiet it. Her thoughts were focused on Samuel and just what perils he would meet in Maine. She wanted to say that she did not understand his reasons for putting himself in danger, but in truth, she could understand him to a degree. There were times that she wished for something more in her life and became unsatisfied with doing the same things all the time. Yet, to get yourself killed for it… that she could not comprehend.

Her thoughts drifted to her brother James, who had died in battle. When she was seven, he went off to fight the natives at Black Point in Maine. She remembered how her mother had doubled over and been brought to weeping upon learning of her son's fate. Her father and John had spoken in hushed tones about how he had died: a shot to his chest near the heart. The wound had proven almost instantly fatal with the poor man bleeding out rapidly. *No, God, please do not let that happen to Sam,* she silently prayed.

Soon the sky grew dark and filled with a spray of stars. She didn't know how long she stayed out there, but it must have been for a long time because Joseph came out and quietly sat beside her. He seemed to have trouble sitting in a comfortable position with his long legs making the task difficult for him. For awhile he said nothing, unsure of how to broach the subject without upsetting her further.

"I came out here to be alone." She broke the silence for him.

"I know, but we started to wonder if you had fallen asleep," he said.

"So what if I had?" she sighed and turned away from him.

Joseph sighed too before getting to the matter at hand. "He will come back."

"You do not know that," she contradicted him.

"Is it not best to be hopeful?" he genuinely asked. "From what I understand, this is mainly a building expedition. I am sure he will be safe."

"As I told him, there is always the possibility of a raid or an ambush." Then she whispered, "James suffered as much."

It pained Joseph still to think of their deceased brother. "James was a sad loss to all of us, but think not so gravely." He tried his best to cheer her. "Think instead of the day when Samuel will return. I think he should fear more of dying from you leaping on him than an Indian attack!"

She couldn't help but giggle as the image of that scene made its way into her head. "Oh but that would be most inappropriate," she spoke in amused sarcasm.

"Only on Sunday."

They both fell into laughter before ceasing to talk. Leaning back against the tree, they looked up and watched the stars blinking in the black sky. They seemed so close, yet they were so very far above them.

"Do you ever wonder what it would be like to be among the stars? To just be able to stare down at the world below? To be greater than everything around you?" Sarah rambled on as she expressed her thoughts aloud.

"It must be what it is like to be in heaven or to be God even, though I would not speak such blasphemy." He sounded far away as if he too was lost in thought.

"Nor I, but I wonder at how it must feel to be something greater than yourself," she mused. "To understand what you could not comprehend otherwise and to do things beyond your current reach."

"What do you mean?" He was confused by her last statement.

"I suppose what I mean is to be able to know everything about the universe, about our world and the invisible world, beyond what we know now. And to use that knowledge to do more than what we are capable of doing. To reach that sort of enlightenment, it must be quite empowering." Her voice was laced with subtle awe.

"Perhaps, but maybe too much knowledge is a dangerous thing," he said in earnest. "You may lose yourself in trying to comprehend more than you are capable of, and if certain things are beyond our doing, it may be because we would use them for harm instead of good."

"Maybe," but the voice inside her head said, *or so we are led to believe*. She did not speak her thought aloud though as she did not want to ruin the placid moment with arguing. Instead, she let the sounds of crickets and leaves rustling in the breeze fill the air as they took solace in the warm summer night.

ଓ

The next day, Sarah was baking bread in the kitchen with her mother. Kneading the dough proved to be a good way to vent her frustrations. She complained to her mother about how she was feeling regarding Samuel.

"Sarah, try not to upset yourself," Mary told her. "Men sometimes wish to prove something to themselves—or others for that matter. I cannot fathom it myself."

"I just wish there were peace among us already so that we would not have to send our men off to die." Then with exasperation, Sarah said, "Oh, war is so tiring."

"Indeed it is, but alas it is the reality in which we live, but all you can do now is pray that Samuel returns."

"He needs to or I may end up an old crone," Sarah muttered.

"Oh stop that, there are other men in this village," Mary reminded her. "Though why you have never looked on any of them I cannot comprehend."

"Because I want no other." And Sarah had never realized that until this moment.

Mary turned abruptly to look at Sarah, and the look in her daughter's eyes confirmed what she had known for awhile now. She sighed. "Yes, I feared you had fallen in love with him."

"I suppose I have," she whispered.

Mary gently touched her cheek. "Then to spare you a broken heart, dear girl, I will pray that he comes home."

"Does this mean you consent to the match?" Sarah smiled then.

"If he were to ask for your hand I may give my consent, although he should ask to formally court you first," she stated.

"I wonder if he never did because he knew he may go off to serve," Sarah thought aloud.

"'Tis possible," Mary replied. "Perhaps he did not want to further stoke your feelings for him should he perish."

Before Sarah could say more, Ann came bursting into the kitchen and spoke hurriedly. "Have you heard? About Joseph Ballard?"

Sarah and Mary exchanged glances, and Sarah asked, "No, what about him?"

"Well, you undoubtedly have heard how his wife has been ill of late?" They nodded. "Now he is certain someone is afflicting her so he has requested that some of the girls from Salem come here. They are to identify who is harming her."

"What?" Mary gasped. "No, he cannot, he will kill

us all!"

"How can you say so?" Ann looked baffled at her sudden outburst.

"Have you not heard about what befell Salem?" she asked incredulously. "Those girls started pointing fingers and then others joined them in accusing their neighbors. Why do you think the same would not happen here?"

"But why be so certain that it would?" Ann retorted. "I think we are not so quarrelsome here that we would turn against our neighbors."

"I already feared the Ballards would come to this, now heed my warning, child." Mary suddenly became grave as she spoke. "Nothing good will come of these girls being brought here." Too aggravated to stay in the room, Mary left the bread she was working on and walked out of the kitchen. Sarah and Ann stood in awkward silence after her exit.

"Do you think she is right?" Ann suddenly looked worriedly at Sarah. "Do you think we would succumb to accusing each other?"

"I cannot say." Sarah shook her head. "I would like to think we would not, but if there truly are witches here, their neighbors may find it their duty to root them out. Though I cannot understand why my mother is so terrified of these accusations. She is not a witch, what would she have to fear?"

"Precisely, and so many are of good repute here that I cannot imagine there should be much for the girls from Salem to find," Ann stated.

"Let us hope not."

CHAPTER FIVE

Like a deadly plague, the witch hysteria swarmed Andover. In addition to the girls from Salem, the afflicted now included Timothy Swan and Sarah Phelps of Andover. It seemed almost every day someone new was being accused and arrested. Mary's fears were confirmed when those accused not only confessed, but started to accuse others as well. It seemed the entire town had fallen into a frenzy with people turning on each other in an instant. To make matters worse, Goody Ballard died from her illness near the end of July, proving to those who believed in the accusations that a witch had indeed killed her.

Sarah started to agree with her mother's point-of-view as more and more people who were normally good, upright citizens were being accused. She found it hard to believe that all of them could be witches. The most she was willing to admit at this point was that witches still hidden among them may have been implicating the accused to the afflicted to cause chaos in their community. Yet, deep within her, something was telling her that there were no witches at all and the accusations were simply the result of hysterical children and the fear that they stoked in others.

Witchcraft was not the only problem Andover faced. At the beginning of August, there had been a raid by some of the Native Americans in Billerica near the Andover border. Several people, even young children, had been slaughtered. Needless to say, this only increased the paranoia within the community. Mary was beside herself, constantly fretting over just when disaster would strike her family. The raid only solidified Sarah's worries for Sam, especially as she had heard nothing from him since he had left.

Near the middle of August, the Parkers received a visit from their cousin Stephen and his mother, also named Mary. John and Joseph welcomed their cousin heartily and Mary gave her sister-in-law a warm hug. Sarah was busy repairing some linens with needle and thread in the next room and put her work aside upon seeing the arrival of her extended family members. She wiped her sweaty hands on her apron as she walked up to her aunt.

"Aunt Mary, how have you fared?" she asked with a smile.

"Oh, well enough," her aunt said as she put a hand on Sarah's face, forcing her cheek into an uncomfortable position. "How pretty you have become, and not yet fattened by childbirth like that sister-in-law of yours." Thankfully Ann was upstairs with her sons and not within earshot.

Aunt Mary gave Sarah a crooked smile before moving on to Peter. Sarah looked with widened eyes at her mother, who only looked at her in sympathy. Their aunt had gained a brusque temperament in her later years and was known to go through periods of mental instability. Sarah looked toward Peter as he was being tormented by his aunt, who was pulling on his arm as if judging how he was growing.

"Yes, you are growing like a weed, just like your brother." She patted his face roughly. He exchanged an annoyed look with Sarah, who only shrugged her shoulders empathetically. Stephen saved them both by taking his mother by the arm and leading her away from her nephew.

"Forgive her," he said. "She lacks in socializing of late, save for at Sabbath service. I thought getting her out of doors and seeing her family for a time would do her good."

"Now you will dictate what I do!" His mother turned on him in an instant. "It is bad enough you have taken my estate from me!"

"I have not taken it from you," he defended himself.

"No, just my control over it!" she yelled back.

"Mother, please, not now," he urged her to stop.

"Afraid they will know what a terrible son I have?" she scolded him.

He pulled her over to a chair and tried to get her to sit. "Please calm yourself before you fall into a swoon," he sighed.

She pulled her arm out of his grip but sat anyway. "I am calm. It is you who causes me upset," she raged as her nostrils flared and her eyebrows knitted together in anger.

They all knew that it was this behavior that caused Stephen to take control over most of his mother's affairs. She was prone to such outbursts and they were often nonsensical. She had also been forgetting things with more frequency and he was afraid she would mismanage the family's estate. His face was red in embarrassment after she had yelled at him. Mary gently touched his arm in reassurance before kneeling in front of her sister-in-law.

Mary took her hands in her own and spoke to her softly. "Would you like to see the children? They grow bigger every day."

"Anything to get away from this child." She pointed accusingly at her son. "I hope you are raising them better than I raised my own."

"Come, we will go see them," Mary stated as she helped her sister-in-law up and the two ascended the stairs.

Stephen hung his head in shame. "I am terribly sorry," he spoke sadly. "I fear every day her condition worsens, but I know not what to do."

"Can no physician help her?" Joseph asked.

"They do not know what ails her," he replied. "All we can do now is make sure she doth not hurt herself or try not to upset her. But even when we do nothing to her she falls into fits yelling and crying about this or that. Why just last night she started raving about witchcraft and specters and it took everything in our power to stop her from crying out against anyone."

"Your mother is not the only one who has taken to being hysterical over witchcraft," John claimed. "Our mother is in constant worry over these accusations."

"Well, how can she not be? When child turns against mother and brother against brother, it is understandable that she would have such fears," Sarah spoke on her mother's behalf.

"It is pure madness that all of these people so readily confess," Stephen agreed.

"Even Reverend Dane's family members are accused and confessing," John said.

"To think the minister's own kin have fallen into the devil's hands," Peter chimed in.

"You cannot truly believe that they have." Stephen gave him an incredulous look.

"Why else would they confess?" Peter asked.

"I have seen firsthand how afraid the accused are and pressured into confessing," Stephen replied. "Between the magistrates and their own family members urging them to confess, it is no wonder that they do."

"And why would their family members want them to confess unless they believe that they were guilty?" Peter continued to question.

"Because everyone seems to be absolutely gripped by fear. They know not how to respond when they are accused, and perhaps they believe that confessing will gain them more sympathy with the court than pleading innocence," Joseph said.

"Do you believe these people are at least afflicted?" Peter turned back to Stephen.

"I believe they may have some illness, but I cannot bring myself to believe that so many people have brought them to such pains," his cousin answered.

"But what—"

"Peter, hush!" Sarah cut him off before he could talk more. She nodded to the stairs where footsteps could be heard.

Aunt Mary and their mother were coming back down and the last thing they needed was for their aunt to have another outburst regarding witchcraft.

"That boy of yours is a delight, John," Aunt Mary said as she came back into the room. "Thank you for showing them to me." She turned to her sister-in-law and squeezed her hand in her own.

"Well, they certainly enjoy seeing you." Mary smiled at her.

Aunt Mary turned back to her son. "Come, Stephen, I wish to return home, I am tired." She used a much softer tone with him now, further proof of her wavering state of mind.

He seemed relieved by it though and bade his family farewell. "Thank you for receiving us."

"You know you are always welcome here," John said as he walked them out.

When they were gone, Mary turned to her children. "That poor woman," she said. "What a sad thing it is for your mind to be in shambles."

"And her family to have to deal with it," Joseph remarked. "Stephen seems to be beside himself."

"I pray for them all that they may be able to bear this burden," Mary spoke quietly.

It was sad truly. None of them knew what had gone wrong in their aunt's mind. Over the years she had slowly started to lose more and more of her composure. And there was seemingly no hope for improvement on the horizon.

CB

The arrests continued through the end of August with more people from Andover being accused. Another round of hangings had also occurred and Martha Carrier was among the executed. The Parkers were all anxious with wondering just who would be accused next and if these accusations would ever end.

Sarah was outside tending to and gathering the herbs. Going over to the rose bush at the end of the garden, she sighed in frustration at seeing the condition of the flowers. They must have become infected with a fungus as their leaves started to turn yellow and black and fall off. The roses themselves had long since lost their petals and no new buds had formed.

"This is horrendous," she muttered, picking off the dead leaves.

"What happened to your roses?" She heard her mother's voice behind her.

"I know not, some disease perhaps," she said in exasperation as she turned toward her mother.

"Oh dear, we will just have to find a remedy for it next year then." Mary held up a piece of paper. "For you, Sarah."

"A letter?" she asked, walking to her mother. "Is it from Sam?"

"It appears so." Mary smiled brightly at her.

Sarah took the letter in her hands and looked it over. For the first time in over a month, she felt genuinely happy. Taking a break from her work and walking under the oak tree, she carefully broke open the seal on the letter. The hand was scratchy and there were some spelling mistakes, but she managed to read it nevertheless. In the letter, Sam apologized for not writing to her sooner for he and the other men were constantly busy. The building of the fort at Pemaquid took up most of his time, but the construction was going faster than he expected. He and some of the other men were also sent out on raids of the local villages, much to his displeasure. At the end of the letter, he reassured her of his safety and said he looked forward to the day when they would be reunited.

She read the letter twice over, making sure she hadn't missed any details. Although he tried to sound cheerful for the most part, his words seemed to be laced with an unspoken sadness. She could not help but wonder if more had happened than what he was telling her. Of course, he could also just be homesick and growing weary with his martial duties. Regardless, she was happy to hear from him, just to know that he had survived to this point. She tried not to think of the possibility that he perished between the time he wrote the letter and when she received it. Still, this letter was the best news she had received in weeks considering all that was going on.

Later that night she decided to write back to him, but was having trouble thinking of what to say. Should she tell him about the witch accusations that were happening, or would that only bring him unneeded worry? Perhaps he already knew. After all, if Governor Phips was with the militia, he would undoubtedly have news brought to him and it would travel among the men. She mulled over these thoughts as she brushed the horses' manes in the stable. It was a comforting task and gave her a chance to be by herself and think. She liked tending to the beautiful animals and they seemed to like the attention. Once Sarah had finished brushing the last horse's mane, she rubbed its nose and the horse nuzzled against her in seeming thanks.

"Yes, you are most welcome." She grinned at the animal. "Goodnight, girl."

Giving the horse one final pat on the back, she walked out of the stables, closing the door behind her. A rustling noise came from behind her and she turned suddenly at the sound. It was later than she realized as it was now completely dark out with only her lantern and the light from the house allowing her to see anything. A breeze picked up and caused a ripple to go through the cornfields. She looked out across the shadowy landscape and was suddenly gripped by an ominous feeling. For some reason, she felt as if she were being watched and wondered just who or what may be hiding out in the darkness. Quickly, she made her way back to the safety of the house.

Shaking off her previous misgivings, she sat at the writing desk to compose a reply to Sam. She started by telling him that she and her family were well, but that she missed him terribly. She had decided to tell him about the witch accusations, but kept it brief and limited the details on the anxiety they gave her. With her eyes growing weary from writing by candlelight, she finished off the letter by saying she hoped to hear more from him and was still praying for him daily. She blew out the candle and headed to bed. That night she had a most pleasant dream of being in a field overgrown with roses with a cool river running through it. It would be the last good dream she would have for a long time.

CHAPTER SIX

September 2, 1692

The morning started as any other would have, but Mary felt a strange discontent within her. She could not explain it, but as soon as she had awakened, she felt more apprehensive than usual. So anxious was she that upon cleaning the table from the morning meal, she dropped one of the pots, spilling the remainder of its contents upon the floor. The sound startled Ann and Sarah, who were helping her clean.

"Mother? Does something ail you?" Sarah raised an eyebrow at her as she knelt to wipe up the mess.

"Forgive me, 'twas but a tremor of the hand." Mary kept her voice low as she knelt beside Sarah to clean the spilled food.

Sarah eyed her carefully as she had noticed her mother's nervous demeanor. All morning she was quieter than normal and her mind seemed not present at all. Sarah wondered if perhaps her mother was coming down with a fever or some other illness. Mary said nothing more on the matter and proceeded to go listlessly about her daily routine. Sarah didn't press her further but decided to keep an eye on her.

John, Joseph, and Peter meanwhile set out to work in the fields. The crops had grown plentiful enough for the family and they were working on gathering the fruits and vegetables. In the distance, the sound of a horse's hooves could be heard. Joseph heard the sound first, and looking out across the fields, could see Constable John Ballard coming up the road toward the house. His breathing became shallower with anticipation.

"Oh dear God, what does he want?" At times such as these, there was only one thing a constable would be coming to their home for.

"It cannot be," John whispered to himself. The brothers walked toward the man and waited in silence until Ballard pulled his horse to a stop before them. "Mr. Ballard," John greeted him sternly. "Why do you come to us this day?"

"Mr. Parker... I fear I have a warrant here to apprehend your mother," he replied.

"Be it for witchcraft?" Joseph asked harshly.

"Yes, the girls have complained of her tormenting them." Ballard seemed to recoil from Joseph's towering form as he spoke.

"Damn them all," Joseph spat. "Our mother has committed no crime."

"Still I must take her."

From inside the house, Sarah saw the group of men conversing together and let her curiosity get the best of her. A chill ran through her body as she stepped outside and saw who the stranger was. "Who doth he come for?" she asked her brothers.

John turned toward her. "He wants to take our mother, but we will not allow it."

"Mother? She is no witch." Sarah was quaking with both fear and anger knowing that there would be no other reason for her arrest. She then felt a presence beside her and turned to see her mother.

"Mother, get back in the house!" John commanded.

"So there was reason for the dread I felt," Mary said quietly, ignoring her son. Her words were not directed at Sarah, however, as she seemed to speak only to herself. She began to walk forward, a distant look in her eyes, and announced, "I will go of my own accord."

"No, you cannot!" Sarah shrieked at her mother's compliance.

"Turn around now!" John yelled at her again.

"Do not command me. Remember I am still your mother." She was firm in her tone with him as if he were still a child.

"But how can you go so willingly, so calmly?" Her eldest son was just as astounded as the rest of the family members.

"It was only a matter of time." She shook her head sadly. "We would have been foolish to think ourselves safe. Delaying the inevitable will only lead to more trouble."

Sarah ran after her and pleaded with Ballard, "Please, sir, you know our mother. You know she would never practice witchcraft. Please, do not take her."

"I have orders I must follow," he muttered in response. With the man's sister-in-law having died recently from what her family believed was witchcraft, he was not ready to hear pleas of innocence.

"Have you no integrity, man?" Joseph rounded on him.

"I must follow the law as we all must!" Ballard reaffirmed his position and with Mary in his custody, he set his horse to a trot and rode off to Salem.

"Make haste; we will follow!" John ordered his siblings and they too prepared to ride to Salem.

⁂

Mary waited anxiously outside of the courtroom of the Salem Town House for her examination to begin. Clenching her hands together, she could feel the sweat building on them. Ballard stood beside her, not saying a word. His face was unreadable and she could not be sure if he thought she was guilty of the charges or not. She heard footsteps coming up the stairs and saw John, Joseph, Peter, and Sarah walk into the hall. She had no time to speak to them, however, as she heard her name called.

"Mary Parker, widow of Andover." One of the magistrates called for her to be brought before them. Ballard took her arm and led her inside. Her children followed and moved along the walls toward the front of the courtroom. The benches were all filled by spectators and only standing room remained. Walking up to the four judges that were present, Mary could see that several of the accusers had fallen down and were writhing and crying out in pain.

"Will you recover them from this affliction?" one of the judges asked Mary, looking at her sternly. If she remembered correctly, this magistrate was John Hathorne.

"But I have not hurt them." Her voice came out more broken and nervous than she intended.

"Lay your hand upon them, you are so commanded," he demanded.

Mary felt cold and clammy as she walked up to the girls, afraid of how they would react, fearing they would condemn her. One by one she touched the five girls who had fallen and one by one each of them recovered from their fits. She recognized several of them, including Sarah Phelps and Mercy Wardwell, who were from Andover. The other members of the Parker family were watching the scene with fearful fascination.

"You are accused of acting witchcraft upon Martha Sprague and Sarah Phelps," Hathorne stated when the girls had finally calmed. "How long have ye been in the snare of the devil?"

In her panicked state, Mary said the first defense that came to her mind. "I know nothing of it. There is another woman of the same name in Andover." She referred of course to her sister-in-law. Mary did not mean for her defense to sound like an accusation, but simply to point out that the officials may have the wrong woman.

"But this is the very woman who hath afflicted me," a voice among the girls called out. Mary turned to see Martha Sprague standing among them. When Sprague saw Mary looking at her, she fell into a fit.

"Recover her!" Hathorne commanded.

Mary did as she was told, but just as Sprague stopped convulsing, Mercy Wardwell once again started to tremble. Mary touched her and her jerking stopped, but then the accuser next to her began to twist and turn and she cried out for Mary to stop hurting her. Before Mary could act, Wardwell fell again. It became chaotic and Mary wondered if their fits would ever cease. She laid her hands upon them both and the girls were finally still.

Mary stood and turned around only to be confronted by William Barker, Jr. "You were with me last night and together we afflicted Martha Sprague," he stated.

"And I saw you afflict Timothy Swan right before my eyes," Wardwell called from behind her, now stable enough to speak.

Mary was dizzy at this point. The constant convulsing of the afflicted and the accusations were more than she could take at any one time. Why had they even brought her name up? It was like an endless nightmare in which any action she took only moved her closer to condemning herself. To make matters worse, one of the girls she had originally recovered from a fit was once again having violent tremors, but this time blood was coming out of her mouth. The magistrates stood up, seeing the girl's worsened condition.

"Mary Warren!" one of the judges called to the girl, but she did not respond. "Help her!" he said to the people near the accusers.

Some of the onlookers ran over to her and checked her over. "Look, she has a pin run through her hand!" a man exclaimed as he held up the young woman's pricked hand. Shocked gasps ran through the crowd.

"Bring her near," the judge ordered. Gingerly, two men managed to get Warren to her feet and slowly walked her over to where Mary stood. "Relieve her of your torment now," the judge spoke coldly to Mary.

With great reluctance, she once again revived the teen with her hand. When she came to, the magistrate asked, "What happened, child?"

"This woman's specter hurt me," Warren answered, staring at Mary with wild eyes. "I remember now that I saw her at an examination at Salem Village. Her spirit was sitting upon one of the beams in the meetinghouse. She frightened me then as she does now!" Warren began to shake and her head drooped forward. The men helped her back to her seat.

"Mary Parker, you have committed detestable acts before us today," Hathorne spoke, commanding all attention back to the front of the courtroom.

"But I have not. They must be mistaken or someone else harms them in my shape." Mary tried in vain to defend herself, but her guilt seemed a sure thing now to the court.

"You still have the audacity to lie after all we have witnessed." He shook his head at her in disappointment. "Take her to the jail immediately."

Mary was shocked and tried to make sense of everything that had just happened. She looked over to her children as one of the officials led her out of the courtroom. The Parkers' faces were a mix of rage, shock, and dejection. Sarah was stunned at the scene she had just witnessed. She felt frozen in place until she felt something rush past her. She turned to see her brothers running out of the courtroom after their mother and she followed them.

Mary was taken to Salem prison. The jailer allowed the Parkers to sit with their mother in the common room before taking her to a cell. Mary was shaking and Joseph sat beside her, an arm wrapped around her shoulders. He used his free hand to hold his mother's, trying to comfort her as best he could.

"I did… I did nothing to them. I swear it." Her voice cracked. "Please, you believe me, do you not?"

"Of course we do," John said softly. "We will not be fooled like so many others into believing what we know not to be true."

"They just started to convulse and… and I knew not what to do but what I was commanded." She broke down into tears then. "I will surely be condemned now."

"No, we will not allow that." Joseph tightened his hold on her. "We will see to it that you are set free."

"But what can you do?" She wiped the tears from her eyes.

"Petition the court or even the governor if we must," he said. "We will establish your innocence."

Sarah was still in shock from what had happened and she didn't know what to say to comfort her mother. She took her hand instead, and her mother looked up at her tearfully. They sat talking for awhile more before the jailer came back to retrieve Mary. John asked him some questions about the conditions in which his mother would be kept. Mary embraced Sarah and Peter before she was taken to a cell. John and Joseph walked with her as she was led away, leaving her two youngest children alone.

Sarah turned to her brother, who looked white as a sheet. "Well, do you still have faith in the truth of these accusations?" she asked sullenly.

He frowned at her but said nothing. A tense silence surrounded the two siblings as they waited for their brothers. After several moments, John and Joseph returned, looking angrier than before. When they were outside of the jail, Sarah asked if something else had happened.

"They put her in goddamn irons," Joseph spat.

"What? Why?" Sarah asked in disgust, ignoring her brother's foul language.

"They do it to all of them," John answered for him. "Apparently her spirit will do mischief without them."

"Horseshit!" Joseph growled as he climbed onto his horse. He held out a hand for Sarah to climb up behind him. She held on tightly as he set the horse to a fast pace in his agitated state and the four of them rode home.

❧

In the days that followed, Sarah found it difficult to concentrate on her daily chores with thinking constantly of her mother suffering in prison. Her absence in the house was unsettling to say the least and Sarah worried herself sick thinking of what may happen to her mother. John and Joseph had gone to visit Mary today and took Ann with them, who wished to see her mother-in-law. This was the second time the brothers had gone since the day of Mary's examination, having taken Peter with them the first time. Sarah had yet to go, fearing she would break down seeing her mother in that condition. She had prepared food for her each time though, a small token to show she still cared as much as ever.

Each time John and Joseph went to see Mary they tried to convince her to confess. They hoped that if she could put on a display of repentance and professed that she wished to be saved from the devil's grip, the court would delay any proceedings against her. Mary vehemently refused to, however, believing that it was better to tell the truth and not condemn her soul than to lie and go to hell for her sin. While they understood their mother in principle, they wished she would not put her life at stake. They preferred her to lie now so that she may live longer and repent later, but she would not be swayed.

John, Joseph, and Ann came home by midday all looking despondent and exhausted. "What news do you bring?" Sarah asked.

"She still refuses to yield," John replied as he sat down at the table. He sighed and leaned back into the chair.

"No matter what we say to persuade her, she will still maintain her innocence," Joseph added as he went to get a cup of ale.

"I blame her not for that, but… doth she not have fear for the worst that may happen?" Sarah asked, not wanting to speak out loud the possibility of the court condemning her.

"She does, but she believes 'tis best for her to speak the truth and die without sin." John shook his head.

"Speak not of her dying," Peter spoke harshly. "She must not perish." He turned abruptly and stomped out of the room.

John got up and went to get some ale for himself as well. Just then, Jacob appeared from around the corner. The little eavesdropper was attentive to the conversations that were taking place in the house of late. He looked quizzically up at his father. "Is it true that Grandmother is a witch? Will she hurt me?" he asked.

John's face turned red and he rounded on his son. "Never speak thus!" he yelled. "Your grandmother is not a witch!"

The little boy's face contorted and he started to cry at bearing the brunt of his father's wrath. Ann went over to her son and wrapped her arms around him. "John, please, he is only a child. He does not understand," she said as she soothed her sobbing child.

John shook his head in exasperation and went out into the yard. Sarah and Joseph exchanged glances, both frightened by their brother's outburst. Clearly, the tension from the current situation was becoming unbearable for all of them.

☙

Later that night in his room, John sat heavily on the bed deep in thought. Ann was brushing out her hair on the other side of the bed and she looked at her husband's tense frame. She felt horrible about everything that was happening, but there was little she could do to remedy the situation.

"I was too harsh with the boy," John finally spoke.

"You certainly scared him," she muttered in response.

"I did not mean to lash out at him," he said softly. "I am just so terribly frustrated. I feel useless to do anything."

She sat beside him and put a hand on his shoulder. "I am sure that this situation will right itself. God will bring your mother's salvation," she comforted. Although deep down, she knew the outcome looked grim.

"I can only pray," he whispered as he turned to her. His eyes were watery and Ann was shocked to see it. Very rarely did her husband show such a display of emotion. "I was taught from a young age that I needed to be strong for my family," he spoke quietly. "When my father died, I rose up to be the head of this family. I was supposed to protect you all and now I have failed."

"No you have not," she said. "What more could you have done?"

"Something, anything…" He trailed off.

"You put too much on yourself," she gently chided him.

What many didn't understand about her husband that she understood perfectly well, was that if he came across as too stern or wanting of joy, it was only because he felt the heavy burden of having to provide for his family and do what he judged was best for them. Any misstep and he was afraid they would suffer. He felt that he was the one who needed to hold them together so that they would prosper. She caressed his cheek as she observed his gloomy face. She pressed her lips to his for a brief moment before resting her forehead against his.

"Perhaps I should have more faith." He gave her a small smile.

"Indeed, you should." She smiled back.

He stared at her for a moment. "You look particularly lovely tonight," he said before kissing her back.

In the next room, Sarah once again found herself in a restless state that night. She spent a long time praying for her mother and Sam before getting under the covers. She felt tired, but everything seemed to bother her and keep her awake, from the wind howling outside to the random creaks that resounded in the house. As she lay trying to find sleep, a strange sound startled her. At first, it sounded as if someone was in pain. The sound was then followed by another one, longer and less pained. Upon recognizing what it was, she rolled her eyes in exasperation. Normally, the couple in the house would keep their intimacies as discreet as possible.

"Now? With all that has been going on?" she muttered to herself in annoyance.

The sounds continued and she got up from her bed. Peeking her head out of her room, she saw Peter standing on the steps, he too awakened by the noise. They both looked at each other with knowing, raised eyebrows. She had a right mind to tell her brother and his wife to keep it the hell down. Luckily, Joseph saved her from the task as he grumbled his way down the attic stairs with an annoyed look on his face .He then proceeded to pound on John's door.

"What the hell are you doing to her in there?" he demanded.

"Damnit, Joseph! Go to bed!" John shouted back at him from behind the closed door.

"I would like to, but your wife's yowling keeps me from sleep!"

"Go away!"

"Perhaps I should find a brothel. I would find better sleep there it seems!"

Sarah and Peter couldn't help but burst into laughter from their brothers' banter. "Joseph, you better stop or my eyes will not be the only thing producing water," Peter managed to get out.

"Don't you dare piss on my floor," Joseph playfully reprimanded him before turning back to the bedroom door. "You hear that, John? You are about to make our poor brother piss himself!"

"Joseph, stop!" Sarah giggled while wiping tears from her eyes.

"Our sister as well!"

Suddenly the bedroom door opened violently, and John stood behind it, trying his best to conceal his nakedness. "All three of you get to bed now, or I will whip you all myself on the morrow."

"Oh, now that is tempting." Joseph wiggled his eyebrows at him teasingly.

John glared at him. "It would be incumbent on you to act your age."

"Then lead thus by example and keep your midnight activities to yourself," Joseph replied saucily.

But upon seeing the look on John's face, he hurried back up the stairs, cackling the entire way. John shot looks at both Sarah and Peter as well and the two hurried back to their respective bedchambers. For as awkward as the moment had been and how embarrassed her poor sister-in-law would be in the morning, Sarah had to admit that she needed a good laugh right now.

CHAPTER SEVEN

By the week of the twelfth, the family had been informed that Mary would have her trial. They were taken aback by just how quickly after her arrest she was to be tried. John and Joseph scrambled to think of defenses for their mother and they were going to see her today to prepare her for her court date. Sarah finally got up the courage to see her mother and went with her brothers. She listened intently as they discussed possible defenses on their way to the prison. They arrived at the gloomy wooden building faster than normal, her brothers having set the horses at a quicker pace in their haste to get to their mother.

If there was one thing Sarah would never forget, it was the smell of Salem jail. Her brothers had insisted on seeing their mother in her cell so as not to be overheard by the jailer. The jailer looked bored to tears with his duties upon their arrival, but his expression changed to annoyance after the brothers asked to see their mother in her cell. Stomping over to a cell on their left, the jailer opened the door and immediately a foul odor permeated the air. It was a mixture of sweat, sour milk, and human feces.

"Dear God," John muttered as they all covered their mouths and noses with their hands.

They walked into the cell, which was partially lit by a small, barred window. The jailer left and closed the door behind them. There were several women in the cell, some of whom were also from Andover. Mary sat in the corner on what looked to be a mat made of straw. Upon noticing her children, she stood and walked over to them. Seeing her mother in shackles broke Sarah's heart. She also noticed that her mother's eyes looked red and puffy like she had been crying.

"Mother," Sarah whispered as she embraced her. "I am sorry I did not come sooner."

With the irons on, Mary was unable to return the embrace fully. "Worry not, you are here now. But am I no longer allowed in the common room?" she asked, turning to her sons.

"We wished to speak with you here so the jailer would not interfere," Joseph said. "Though I think we made a mistake. It smells of filth in here."

"You get used to it after awhile." Mary shrugged

"Are you aware that you are to be tried this week?" John asked.

"Yes, I have been informed," she spoke sadly.

"We need to prepare your defense and go over everything we know about the accusations against you," he continued.

"As if it will come to any good," she sighed. "More were condemned last week."

"Regardless, we must prepare you accordingly," he said. "We know Martha Sprague and Sarah Phelps already accused you and the afflicted at your examination will undoubtedly give testimony."

"And there is also Mercy Wardwell, who said I afflicted Timothy Swan," she added. "William Barker, Jr. also accused me of hurting Sprague." Mary looked thoughtful for a moment before adding, "Do you think Moses Tyler put it in Sprague's head to accuse me? He is after all her stepfather."

"It is possible," John replied. "I never trusted that man."

"Why would he do that?" Sarah asked.

"Because of what happened with his brother's apprenticeship," John stated. "Did you never hear Father speak of it?"

Sarah tried to go back through her memories. "I vaguely remember him mentioning it when Hannah got married and he talked of not trusting the Tylers, but I cannot recall what it was about."

"You would not, as it was before you were born. It was about thirty years ago now. Moses's brother Hopestill was apprenticed to Thomas Chandler and your father kept the written contract of his apprenticeship in the house," Mary explained. "The Tylers wanted to break Hope out of his apprenticeship, so they stole the paper from the house when your father and I were out of doors and burned it. Your father testified against them and Hope had to return to Chandler."

"They would still hold it against us? When he is the one who did wrong?" Sarah asked.

"He may still be bitter about it," John added. "Though the man must be more malicious than I thought if he allows his stepdaughter to accuse his own family members."

"But then why would Chandler's granddaughter cry out against Mother? We did naught to them," Joseph questioned. He was referring to Sarah Phelps, who was Chandler's granddaughter.

"Maybe the Chandlers took it as a slight when your sister married into the Tyler family," Mary added. "Perhaps they thought we approved of their previous misdeeds."

"Well, that would make them spiteful, pathetic people, just like the rest of the accusers," Joseph grumbled.

"Which brings us back to the reason for our visit: your trial. We need to discuss defenses," John reminded them. "First as to the afflicted girls, I think you should stress the point of someone hurting them in your shape, be it the devil or another witch," John said.

"But they cared not to hear it the first time," she retorted.

"I know, but press upon the point, even bring up scripture if you must," he urged her.

"Yes, like the witch of Endor and the summoning of Samuel before Saul." Joseph brought up a biblical example for her to use.

Mary thought some more of how to refute the claim of her spirit hurting the afflicted and said, "Perhaps I can also suggest that their fits cloud their vision and they cannot truly see who harms them. They are so desperate to stop the pain that they will bring up any name they can think of."

"But what of your touch stopping their torment?" Joseph pushed back on the point as he took a seat on a bench by the wall.

Mary paused for a moment before speaking again.

"Maybe my touch scares off the spirit that is harming them. Hath it not been said that when others have struck at the place where these spirits supposedly are that the afflicted claimed they disappeared?"

"That is true... good, very good," John remarked.

Joseph moved on to the next point. "Now what of Wardwell and Barker?"

"I will simply say that they were solely responsible for harming Sprague and Swan and now they want to lay the blame at my feet." Her tone was bitter. "After all, as far as I know, they have no one to agree with them on those accusations."

Joseph looked to John, who nodded and said, "Yes, that seems fair enough."

Sarah, who had been listening silently, spoke up. "But what if Sprague confirms that what Barker says is true?"

"Then I shall return to my previous defenses," Mary answered.

"I think we have covered enough regarding the afflicted, what of the claim that you are the devil's servant?" John inquired.

Mary answered immediately with, "I will affirm that I have never sought out the devil and I have only ever loved God."

"And that you have no desire to condemn your soul to hell for such little reward," Joseph added.

"You should also tell them that you have always been of good repute within the community and have never had suspicion of witchcraft upon you before," Sarah chimed in.

"Yes, and that I would have no reason to use witchcraft now," Mary agreed.

They talked some more about possible defenses

as they thought of them. After a lengthy discussion, they felt secure in Mary being prepared enough for her trial. Still, they feared that regardless of how well crafted her defenses would be, the jury would bring her in guilty. It seemed every trial that had occurred thus far ended with the accused being condemned and it gave them little hope that Mary's would end any differently.

John, fearing the worst outcome, pleaded with her once more. "If the worst happens and you are found guilty, if you were to confess it may save your life. I know you think it is a sin, but surely God would forgive you this sin given the duress you face."

"And what if God is testing my conviction now?" she asked. "I will not fail by bearing false witness against myself. I will hear no more of confessing." John shook his head and sighed, knowing there would be no changing her mind.

Mary looked down at her chained hands. "Whatever happens, know that I stood firm against falsehood. That I did not fall before injustice," she announced.

"But at the price of your life…" Sarah said softly as her voice cracked.

"Do you think my life so important? I am one woman, in a world full of people. I am of no great significance," she said.

"You are to us!" Joseph exclaimed. "How can you think so low of yourself? Do you give up on your life so readily?"

"I do not and I will stand before the entire court and profess my innocence," she explained. "But I speak the truth as to my purpose. I believe that I was placed on this earth to bring you all into this world and to raise you to be good, caring people; to be what God truly intended of humanity. I accomplished that and now I am no longer needed here. But I am so proud of all of you, truly I am." Tears formed in her eyes and her voice became strained. "Now you and your children, you must lead the world out of this darkness and into the light."

"But Mother, we still need you." John barely spoke above a whisper.

Mary gently touched her son's face. "You will carry on as you always do. You have grown into such a strong man. Your father would be so proud of how you have taken care of our family in his absence."

They were all openly weeping now. Mary brought all of her children close to her, holding them tight in her arms as if they were still the toddlers she remembered so fondly. After they finally departed, she cried to herself for awhile more. It took everything in her power to compose herself and mentally prepare for her trial. Resting against the rough wooden walls of the jail, she went over her defenses repeatedly, thinking of every way that the accusations against her may go. It was only when she was thoroughly exhausted and stressed beyond her capabilities that she found sleep.

ଔ

September 16, 1692

Mary sat anxiously inside the courtroom waiting for her trial to begin. She felt sick to her stomach and lightheaded with all the stress she had been under. Telling herself to breathe, she went over the defenses in her head once more. She was able to speak with her children briefly before the trial began. They went over what to say with her one last time before she was left on her own.

The courtroom was packed with people, making it hot and stuffy despite the breezy September weather. On the side of the room opposite Mary were the afflicted and her other accusers. The afflicted seemed to be perfectly fine now, all conversing among themselves. Next to them in their assigned section were the members of the jury. They were all men that she did not recognize and they looked none too compassionate. After a long wait that only increased her nervousness, several magistrates walked in and sat down at the front of the room. They were stern-faced and some of them looked dismissive about the trial they were about to preside over.

The chief magistrate, William Stoughton, sat in the middle and began the day's proceedings. "Today presented before us will be the case of Mary Parker, widow of Andover," he announced before turning to the jury. "The court will note that the indictment against the prisoner for afflicting Martha Sprague has been returned ignoramus."

Mary looked back at her children, confused as to why that particular charge had been dropped. They looked back at her equally confused. She then tried to spot Sprague in the crowd, but she was nowhere to be seen. Her absence led Mary to assume that she had failed to attend court and give testimony in support of her accusation and that was why that indictment had not been upheld.

Mary returned her attention to the front of the room as Stoughton addressed her. "Mary Parker, please rise." She did as he ordered and he continued, "You are charged with practicing witchcraft in the town of Andover and using acts of witchcraft on or about the last day of August to afflict, torture, and torment one Sarah Phelps, single woman of Andover. You are likewise charged with using acts of witchcraft on or about the first day of September to afflict, torture, and torment Hannah Bigsby of Andover, the wife of Daniel Bigsby. How do you plead to these indictments?"

Mary was surprised that now Hannah Bigsby, who was Phelps's aunt, had accused her as well. Disregarding her surprise, she gave her plea. "Not guilty."

"Then how do you put yourself upon trial?" he asked.

She answered with the standard response, "By God and my country."

"The following men have been called to serve as members of the jury," he said and then proceeded to read a list of names to her. "Do you object to any of them serving on the trial jury?"

She wanted to have all of them replaced, but knew that, save from her own family members, it would not matter who sat on the jury. "No, I do not," she replied.

"Very well, members of the jury will be sworn in," he continued. She had to wait for each one to be sworn in before the proceedings continued. When the swearing-in was finally finished, Stoughton spoke once again. "Trial will now commence. The prisoner will come to the bar."

Mary moved to stand in the space beside the judges and turned to face the rest of the courtroom.

Seeing so many people watching her made her more anxious. Her hands became sweaty and she was filled with grim anticipation as the trial began.

"Sarah Phelps, come forward," Stoughton ordered. Phelps was a mousy-looking girl of about ten. She cautiously approached the magistrates as if she was afraid of them.

Stoughton questioned her. "Sarah Phelps, you swore before the Grand Inquest that on the last day of August, Mary Parker afflicted you and continued to do so on the day of her examination. You also saw her afflict Hannah Bigsby and Martha Sprague. Do you still swear this to be the truth of what you know?"

"I do, sir," she replied.

"Will you relate to the jury just how she afflicted you?" he questioned.

"On the last day of August, her spirit came before me and forced me to get up from my bed," she explained. "She poked at me and pinched me so that I would not stop moving until I was terribly sore and so tired that I almost fell down dead."

He continued his inquiry. "And what did she do to you upon the day of her examination?"

"She looked upon me and struck me down. Her hands came upon my throat and she choked me," she answered in a pitiful tone.

"Goody Parker, what do you have to say in your defense?" Stoughton turned to Mary.

"I did not afflict her. I believe her fits so belied her senses that she could not see who harmed her and in desperation cried out my name," she answered him.

"But it was you, I know it was! I could see you!"

Phelps cried out.

"Dear child, I remember when you were born and I have never brought harm to you before," Mary said gently to the girl. "What reason would I have for harming you now?"

"Because the devil bids you to," the girl said sheepishly.

"I have only ever put my faith in God, I have no reason to go to the devil now," Mary tried to explain.

"And what God do you put faith in?" Hathorne, who was also present, asked of Mary.

"The same God as you," she said defiantly.

"I think not," he retorted.

Stoughton turned back to Phelps and resumed the questioning. "Now Miss Phelps, how did you see her afflict Hannah Bigsby?"

"I saw Goody Parker strike my aunt in the stomach when we were at Sabbath meeting," she answered. "She had to sit from the pain. Even upon the Sabbath she gives us no rest."

"I would never disrespect the Lord in such a way by doing evil upon the Sabbath," Mary declared.

"Oh, but you do!" Phelps then started to snivel and she burst into tears. "Please do not make me continue," she pleaded to the judges. "I fear she will harm me if I say more."

"But I have never harmed you," Mary countered.

"Oh, I cannot! Please stop! Please!" Phelps began to writhe in place, looking like she was nearing another fit.

"You may return to your seat, Miss Phelps," Stoughton told her. The girl nodded and shakily returned to her place where she was comforted by an older woman.

Stoughton then called up the next accuser. "Hannah Bigsby, please come forward." A woman of average height and build walked up to the bar. She looked haggard and displeased about having to give testimony.

"Goodwife Bigsby, you likewise swore before the Grand Inquest that near the first day of September Mary Parker afflicted you," Stoughton stated.

"She did, sir," Bigsby confirmed in a low voice.

"How did she afflict you?"

"I was at home at work in the kitchen when I was forcefully thrust into the wall. I looked up and saw Goody Parker's spirit. She pushed on my chest so hard that I could not find breath," she stated calmly. "It was not until my husband came forth and drove her from me that I found relief."

He prompted her further. "And did she torment you at any other time?"

The woman elaborated on the story her niece had given earlier. "Once upon the Sabbath, she struck me in the stomach while at meeting for telling the truth of her torments, and pain welled up within my body." Her voice became stronger as she continued, "So great was the pain I could no longer stand and feared I would faint."

Stoughton turned to Mary. "Do you deny her claims as well?"

"I do, for as I said before, I believe she knows not who harms her given how violently afflicted she is," Mary responded. "I also believe it is possible that the devil or another witch appears in my shape to harm her and the others."

"But your consent would be needed for anyone to conjure your spirit," he retorted.

"Did dead Samuel give consent to be raised before Saul?" she contradicted him.

A murmur fell over the crowd at hearing this defense. From where they sat, the Parker siblings could hear some people agreeing with what Mary said. Even some members of the jury seemed to nod their heads in agreement. For a brief moment, they were filled with hope that maybe this trial would conclude in Mary's favor.

"But how do you know he did not?" Hathorne countered.

"That is exactly what I mean. You cannot know one way or the other whether consent was given, so I do not think the appearance of my spirit can be called into evidence against me," she pressed hard against him. "I certainly know I gave no consent to anyone to conjure my spirit."

"Then you have appeared before me as yourself entirely," Bigsby spoke up. "For you now do the devil's work."

"Goody Bigsby, have you ever heard suspicion of witchcraft upon me before this past month?" Mary asked her.

"I cannot say that I have," she replied with a touch of haughtiness to her voice.

"And have I not previously always been an upstanding member of our community and most Christian in heart?" Mary asked further.

"I suppose," was her curt reply.

"Then I ask again, what could bring me to the devil now?"

"He must offer you something."

"What could he offer me that would be worth damning my soul to hell for?"

"I know not…" The woman's resolve seemed to fade after her exchange with Mary.

"She would not know what the devil hath promised you in secret," Stoughton interjected. "Do you have more to say, Goodwife Bigsby?"

"No, your Honor." She looked relieved that he had ended Mary's intense questioning.

"Then you may step down," he said and Bigsby gladly returned to her seat. "William Barker, Jr. come before the prisoner."

The teenager came before Mary and she could not help but feel contempt for him. While part of her believed there may have been something wrong with the afflicted to give them cause to cry out against someone, she found no excuse for one accused person to condemn another. The young man seemed not to notice Mary's dislike of him as his face remained stoic as he approached the bar.

"Mr. Barker, you swore before the Grand Inquest that the night before you confessed on September first, Mary Parker was among your company and afflicted Martha Sprague with you," Stoughton said to him. "Do you recall how the prisoner afflicted Sprague?"

"She, like myself, clenched her hands together and in so doing caused great pain to Sprague," he answered. "She also urged me to continue to afflict Sprague that night and I did so."

"Did Parker afflict Sprague at any other point?"

"At her examination, when she looked upon Sprague, I saw her spirit go from her body and strike the girl down," he testified.

"And what else do you know of Parker being a witch?"

"She and I both rode upon a pole to be baptized at Five Mile Pond by the devil. He dipped her head into the water as he did mine and said that she was his forever and ever," he declared. "This is how I know Goody Parker to be a witch."

Stoughton looked to Mary now. "You have renounced your Christian baptism by covenanting with the devil."

He did not say it as a question, but Mary refuted the claim. "I would never. I have given my soul unto the Lord alone. I am not the witch he claims I am."

"But how could he give such precise details as to your unholy baptism then if you are not a witch?" Hathorne took over the questioning at this point.

"He has a fanciful imagination," she snapped, growing tired of these false claims against her.

"Doth he imagine you afflicting Sprague as well?"

"I believe he *alone* afflicted her and now brings up my name to cast all the blame on me and away from himself." She was harsh in her reply as she turned toward Barker.

"Do you call me a liar?" Barker spat at her.

"Indeed you are!" she exclaimed.

"Then why did Martha Sprague affirm that you afflicted her?"

"Perhaps you threatened her to say so." Mary's anger was boiling over. "After all, why is she not here today to testify to the truth of your statement?"

"She is too ill to stand before us!"

"Or maybe you are afflicting her as we speak to keep her quiet!"

"Enough of this!" Stoughton's voice boomed, silencing them at once. "Mr. Barker, return to your seat."

The teen snarled at Mary before sharply turning and stomping back to the benches. She inhaled deeply, trying to calm herself, but her heart was racing with adrenaline. While she had been despondent and nervous before, now she was furious at how foolish these accusations against her were. The magistrates gave her no relief as they seemed to believe every word that came from these accusers' lips. She was realizing that she had never stood a chance in the first place; her guilt was already a fact in their minds.

"We have one last witness to stand before us today," Stoughton announced. "Mercy Wardwell, come forward." The girl, in her late teens, walked up to them and stood before Mary. "Mercy Wardwell, you swore that you saw the shape of Mary Parker when you afflicted Timothy Swan and Martha Sprague. Did you also see Parker afflict them at that time as well?"

"No, but she did afflict Martha Sprague at her examination," she replied.

"How did she afflict Sprague?"

"She looked upon Sprague and struck her down. Then I saw Goody Parker's shape shaking Sprague for crying out against her."

"Did you also see her afflict either Sarah Phelps or Hannah Bigsby?"

"I saw her afflict Sarah Phelps at her examination. She struck her down and nearly choked her to death," Wardwell responded.

Another judge that Mary recognized from her examination questioned her now. "Goodwife Parker, do you claim that she lies as well?"

"Yes, for she admits to hurting these people and now wants to say that I do the same, so we already know that she hath the capacity to be malicious and fraudulent," Mary explained. "And it is quite possible that she harms them in my shape or forces them to say that I afflict them."

"You afflicted me as well at your examination." The teen defended herself.

"You claim that I was in your company when you afflicted others, why would I now turn on you if we are supposed to have shared the same goal?"

"Because I now tell the truth about you," she answered. "You want to avenge yourself and your spirit attacked me at your examination."

"It could very well have been anyone attacking you," Mary contradicted her.

"Did your touch not recover the afflicted out of their fits?" Hathorne asked Mary.

"I believe it was my touch that scared off the spirit that was afflicting them," she countered.

Suddenly, Wardwell hunched over and clutched at her stomach. "Oh, Goody Parker, you torment me now! Please stop!"

"You bring her to harm before us?" Stoughton rounded on Mary.

"I do not!" she retorted. "I am trying to prove my innocence, why would I appear to her now and condemn myself?"

Before he could respond the rest of the afflicted that were present began to writhe and cry out. One fell from the bench where she sat and onto the floor, twisting this way and that. The members of the jury rose from their seats to look closer at them. Any people who were near to them tried to comfort them and cease their fits.

"Will you stop this torment?" Stoughton looked

back at Mary.

"I cannot, for I do not afflict them!"

"Then you will let them suffer?" He gaped at her.

A throng of cries resounded in the courtroom as the afflicted whimpered and shrieked: "Please stop this torture!" "Uh, I cannot breathe!" "Ah! She claws at my throat!" Their wailing rose to a cacophony and one voice could not be distinguished from another.

"Mary Parker, you will lay your hand upon them now!" Stoughton demanded.

"But I do not harm them!" she screamed in response to be heard over their cries.

"Then you will be forced to relieve them." He gestured for the bailiff to come forward. "Take her to them and have her lay hands upon them."

The man came and grabbed Mary roughly by the arm and led her over to where the afflicted girls were. He forced her to place her hands upon them. Just as at her examination, one by one they ceased to convulse and became calm once more. Mary looked over to her children with frightened eyes and they looked just as fearful as she did. She felt the bailiff pull her arm and she realized she was being led back to the bar.

Mary stood staring at her shaking hands as Stoughton instructed the jury. "Members of the jury, Mary Parker stood before you today charged with using sundry acts of witchcraft to torture, afflict, consume, pine, waste, and torment Sarah Phelps of Andover on the last day of August and Hannah Bigsby of Andover on the first day of September as well as on diverse other days. You have heard the evidence against the prisoner and have heard the testimony from several witnesses. The prisoner has given her defense, but I believe the afflictions we have all witnessed here today stand as testament to the truth of the evidence against her. You are to go from the courtroom and deliberate on the facts of the case as presented to you. When you have reached a verdict on each of the indictments, you will come back to the courtroom and return your verdict. You may now go out to deliberate."

The members of the jury stood and filtered out of the courtroom. The fear Mary felt when recovering the afflicted surged into full panic knowing her fate would soon be decided. She felt a fluttering in her stomach as she worried that the verdict would not be in her favor. She looked at her children, who were aggressively talking amongst themselves. She wanted to go to them but did not think she was allowed to. Instead, she clasped her hands together and sent up a fervent prayer.

Meanwhile, Joseph and John were talking briskly in harsh whispers. "She fought well and said everything she could have. She did everything right," Joseph said.

"She did, but nothing she said will sway the jury after witnessing those fits," John rasped.

"Then they are not fit to serve if they believe that is evidence enough!"

Sarah wasn't listening to her brothers' conversation. Instead, she was glaring at her mother's accusers. They seemed quite healthy and content now, talking among themselves like a chattering pack of mindless birds. They had killed her mother. She knew it deep down and they seemed to not have a single regret about doing so. Her vision was red with hatred and thoughts of violence against the afflicted swarmed into her head as bees swarm a hive.

"Sarah, Sarah!" The sound of John's voice managed to break her trance. "You are going to hurt yourself." He nodded to her clutched hand.

She hadn't realized how tightly she had been holding onto her skirt and her hand was cramping by the time she relaxed it. Her jaw muscles also ached from how hard she had clenched her teeth together. Forcing her attention away from the accusers, Sarah looked at her mother, who was praying. Mary briefly turned her eyes up and locked gazes with her daughter. Sarah mouthed the words "I am with you" and Mary nodded in unspoken understanding.

After several more moments, the jury returned to the courtroom. A sober quiet fell over the room as they made their way back to their seats. Mary felt sick looking at their grave faces, fearing the worst.

Stoughton addressed the foreman. "Mr. Fisk, has the jury reached a verdict on the indictments in this case?"

"We have, your Honor," he replied.

"State your verdict before the court," he commanded.

The foreman spoke. "As to the indictment against Mary Parker for the use of witchcraft to afflict Sarah Phelps and as to the indictment for the use of witchcraft to afflict Hannah Bigsby, we, the members of the jury, find the prisoner *guilty* on both counts."

Mary stopped breathing for a moment, feeling as if the air had been forced from her lungs. She squeezed her eyes shut as Stoughton continued in an unemotional, routine manner, "The verdict being returned guilty, the sentence as the law directs shall be death by hanging."

Mary felt numb, not believing what she had just heard. The courtroom suddenly filled with unintelligible noise as the world around her fell away. The only sound she heard above the din was that of Joseph shouting, "You bastards!" He nearly lunged forward but was held back by John. And then there was Sarah, who looked at no one as her face became dark with wrath.

છ

Sarah stormed upstairs to her room once the family returned home. For a moment she breathed heavily before spotting her hairbrush on the bedside table. She grabbed it and violently threw it against the wall where it made a loud bang. She didn't care that she had left a noticeable dent in the white plaster.

"God damnit!" she roared as she let out all of her anger. She screamed and trembled with rage. "Why?" she asked in harsh contempt as she looked up at the ceiling, speaking to the invisible God above her. "Why are you letting this happen to her?"

She then heard knocking at her door followed by John's voice. "What happened? Are you hurt?"

"I am fine," she bit back.

After some time, she could hear his footsteps retreating from her door. When he was gone, she threw herself onto her bed and screamed into her pillow. Her throat was becoming hoarse and she felt the veins in her neck protruding. Her pulse point throbbed with the fiercely moving blood that rushed through her body. She stayed in her room for several hours and when Ann called for dinner, she refused to go down, too sick with rage to eat.

It was not until night had fallen that she had calmed enough to go downstairs. She found her brothers in deep concentration around the table. "Well, have we arrived at a plan of action?" she asked cynically.

"Depends, do you have any viable ideas?" John replied.

"I thought you spoke of petitioning?" She recalled their previous conversation with their mother.

"To whom? The very people that condemned her?" he spat. "Others have tried to write petitions only for the court to ignore them."

"Then send it to the damn governor if you must," she spoke with an edge to her voice.

"He is still in Maine. By the time he would receive anything and return with a reply, it would be too late." He shook his head. "And besides, you are assuming he would even care. He has never lifted a finger to stop this madness before."

"Then what are we going to do?"

"Short of breaking her out of prison and having her escape all the way to New Jersey, there is not much we can do," Joseph broke in. "So I propose we all get drunk. Perhaps it will lead to a grand epiphany."

He went for a bottle of rum, only to have his older brother reprimand him sarcastically. "Yes, that will be most helpful."

"Well, until you can come up with something useful, I do not plan on going through this ordeal sober," Joseph shot back and proceeded to fill his cup to the brim.

Sarah sighed as her brother took a long swig. "So we are just going to do nothing?"

"What do you want us to do, Sarah?" John's voice turned angry. "We are one family trapped by an entire legal system."

"And what of the other families? Many were condemned recently. If we all worked together we may be able to accomplish something," she suggested.

"Yes, work with the same families who accused our mother who accused their own family members who then accused others who were condemned," Joseph rambled on as he pointed to an invisible diagram in front of him. "I would no sooner go to those people to toss a bucket of piss on me if I were on fire."

"And they would probably be so afraid of retaliation by the accusers and the court that they would agree to nothing anyway," John said.

"Will we just let her die then?" she asked bitterly

"Sarah, enough!" John halted her in exasperation. "I am not the son of God. I cannot work miracles."

He turned from them both and walked upstairs. Joseph pushed the rum bottle toward Sarah. She stared at it for a moment before deciding that the current situation warranted leaving sobriety behind for awhile.

CHAPTER EIGHT

Sarah's conscience did not allow her to sit idly while her mother waited to die. She needed someone outside of her family to give her guidance. It was Sunday and the meetinghouse looked emptier. So many people from their town had been imprisoned that empty spaces in the pews could now be discerned. She sat beside her sisters with Hannah nearly in tears as she related more upsetting news.

"My sister-in-law and her daughter Joanna were examined the same day Mother was condemned," Hannah choked out.

"Yes, I have heard." Elizabeth rubbed her arm in sympathy.

"It was a most devastating turn of events," Hannah continued. "They, with other accused persons, were brought here before the afflicted. They were blindfolded and made to recover the afflicted from their fits. Our brother-in-law bade them confess and they did just to make him relent."

Elizabeth spoke in exasperation, "It hurts my soul

to see so many families torn apart by their members turning on each other."

"Daniel is so angry at his brother for not curbing that Sprague girl," Hannah said softly so as not to be overheard. "But he is afraid to say anything to him because he does not want either myself or any of our children to be accused."

Elizabeth nodded. "I can understand that, especially with so many of your family members already accused."

"I am terrified that I will lose them all," Hannah sobbed as she patted a handkerchief to her eyes.

"The fools sitting on the court may see to it that your fears are justified," Sarah muttered. She felt numb at this point. So many accusations had been hurled and executions performed that by now they no longer surprised her and she was just exhausted from hearing about them.

While every Sabbath service was hard for her to suffer through, this one was particularly trying. She was determined to speak with Reverend Dane after mass ended to hear his opinion on her present dilemma. That was all she could focus on and the mass seemed to drag on forever, taking its toll on her patience. After what seemed an eternity, the service finally ended and she waited behind as everyone filtered out of the meetinghouse. She waited for a few parishioners to finish speaking with the elderly minister before approaching him.

"Miss Parker, I wish I could greet you under more pleasant circumstances," he said when he saw her.

"Yes, and I am sorry for your own family's misfortunes," she replied, acknowledging that his daughter had been condemned the day after her mother. "But Mr. Dane, I know not what to do. My mother has been condemned for a crime she is innocent of and I cannot bear for her to hang for it."

"I have known your mother for many years, and you need not plead her innocence to me for I know it well," he replied kindly. "But I fear I have no help to offer you aside from petitioning the court."

"My brother says others have tried it and it has always failed," she explained.

"Indeed, I have heard the same." He sounded tired, as he too was suffering from this enduring witch hunt. "I would like to offer you better guidance, young Sarah, truly I would. But alas, my own daughter has been condemned and there is not much I can do to sway the court one way or another."

"But I cannot let my mother die." Her voice started to break.

"You may still try to write all the letters and petitions that you can, but if it comes to naught, then you may have to accept the outcome however detestable it may be," he advised. "The Lord often creates plans for which we can see no reason at the moment, only for it to be revealed to us later."

Sarah stood back, appalled and disappointed. Was this the best he had to offer? Just let her mother die because it was God's will? She refused to see his reasoning, convinced that God would have no hand in her mother's death for it was the result of malicious and ill-content people. Breaking her mother out of prison was starting to look more and more like an appealing option as she was sure her family would find no help elsewhere.

Taking a moment to decide what to say to the minister, she said curtly, "I will think more about what to do. Good day, sir."

He gave her an apologetic look as he replied, "I will pray for your mother's deliverance."

She nodded and thanked him before briskly walking away. As she silently fumed all the way home, she felt even more dejected and hopeless than before. She was frustrated with how limited her options were to change the present circumstances and there was little chance that any of them would work. The familiar tension rose in her stomach again as her worry built and she knew she would be too sick to eat again that night. In place of food, she prayed harder than she ever had once alone in her room.

☙

The day for Mary's execution had been set for that Thursday. The entire family went to go see her the day before as John needed to clear up some matters of estate, but most importantly they would be saying goodbye to her. It would be the last time any of them were able to speak with her. Sarah felt like someone had driven a sharp knife into her soul as that fact came into her mind. She thought about just how unfair the whole ordeal was. Her mother was a good, pious woman with a great heart. Sarah's own heart broke knowing that her mother was to suffer a fate she did not deserve. *Why her?* she thought. *Such grave injustice, 'tis not fair... this is so wrong.* A terrible hopelessness filled Sarah as she realized there was nothing she could do to save her mother's life. It pained her to think of just how powerless she was to right the situation. Something akin to hysteria at the thought of her mother's impending death filled her and she wanted to scream with a raging passion for them to not kill her.

Intense grief filled her as she watched the poignant scene of her mother saying goodbye to her grandchildren in the common room of Salem prison. John had not wanted them to come, but Ann insisted that Mary deserved to see them one last time. Likewise, even if the boys would not understand the entire truth or gravity of their grandmother's demise, they needed some sort of closure with her. Jacob, being the inquisitive child that he was, bombarded his grandmother with questions.

"Why are you wearing these?" he asked, tugging at the chains on her wrists.

"They say if I do not, I will harm people," Mary tried explaining lightly, but the bitterness could be heard in her voice.

"*Do* you harm people?" he asked timidly.

"No, little one, I do not, but they do not believe me," Mary said, and it sounded as if she would start crying.

"Mama said you are going to go far away tomorrow, will you ever come back?" He too sounded sad.

A tear rolled down Mary's face and she inhaled sharply to keep her composure. "I will not, but I will always be with you in your heart," she said, touching his cheek tenderly. "And one day, many, many years from now, you and I will see each other again."

"I will miss you." He looked up at her with big sorrowful eyes.

"And I you." She held him tight to her as more tears fell from her eyes.

Sarah had to turn away from the heart-wrenching

scene as she started to sob. She felt as if she would shatter if she had to endure this unbearable situation any further. Behind her, she heard her mother and Ann exchanging farewells before her sister-in-law took the children outside.

Joseph's voice could be heard softly as he tried to not let the jailer hear. "This is your last chance to flee, you know."

"First you wished me to confess and now you want me to escape," Mary replied. "Confessing failed to save Mary Lacey and Ann Foster, who were condemned anyway. And I will not flee. That would leave you all vulnerable and I cannot put you in danger."

He nodded solemnly as his eyes grew watery. "You only ever thought of us, hardly ever of yourself," he sighed.

"That is a mother's duty," she explained to him. "Her children always come first."

"You have been a most dutiful mother," he spoke brokenly. "We were truly blessed to have been your children."

"And what a blessing you all were." She took his hand and patted it affectionately. She turned toward Peter, who was standing against the wall, a distant look in his eyes. "Come here, Peter," she said, holding out her other hand.

He walked over and placed his hand in hers. "Mother…"

"You are my youngest child," she said gently. "Look to your brothers now and help them for you will all need each other dearly in the dark days to come."

He nodded. "I will."

"I know one day you will grow to be as great a man as they." She let go of their hands and pulled her youngest son down to her level and kissed the top of his head. "You are a wise boy; use that wisdom to grow to your full potential."

"And not be a burden to my brothers?" he asked with a small smirk.

"You will be no burden, Lord knows we will have enough of them though," John answered in a tired voice.

"And you must rest," Mary said, turning to her eldest son. "You are exhausting yourself with all that you have undertaken."

"You sound like my wife," John sighed.

"She is a sensible woman, now heed our advice." She squeezed his shoulder. "You have done enough."

But he didn't agree. "If I had done enough, you would be at home now."

"You cannot change what is beyond your control," she replied. "Now hush, I will hear no more of you blaming yourself."

She spoke with her sons some more, before turning to her daughter. "Sarah," she said quietly to the younger woman who was still turned around. Sarah slowly looked over her shoulder at her mother. Upon seeing her daughter's tear-stained face, Mary spoke to her sons. "Please give me a moment with your sister." They did as she asked, moving toward the opposite end of the room as Mary walked over to Sarah. "Oh my poor girl," she sighed. "So this is really the last time we shall speak, is it not?"

Sarah cried more and shook her head. "This is not fair, you... you do not deserve this. I cannot bear to see them kill you."

"And I do not want to die," Mary sadly agreed, her vision starting to blur with unshed tears. "It sickens me so to even think that tomorrow will be my last day on earth. I am not ready to go. But if God wishes to call me home, I suppose I must not impinge on his will. Clearly, I have served the purpose he set out for me, and now I must go. I just wish he had allowed me a more suitable fate."

"Do not we all?" Sarah could feel the heat rising in her face as the anger welled up within her again. "All who accused you should burn in hell."

"Please do not harbor such hatred," Mary said, wiping away Sarah's tears with her thumbs. "You are too young to be so bitter."

"How can I not be with what they are doing to you?" she retorted.

"It is unjust, I know, but holding a grudge will only harden your heart," Mary gently explained. "You have too much to look forward to in your future to feel thus and I will always be with you regardless if I am on this earth or not. Think of the good things to come, like your marriage to Samuel one day."

Sarah was sullen in her reply. "If he even comes home."

"He will; please keep hope in that at least," Mary implored her.

But Sarah only shook her head sadly. "It is so hard to have hope for anything now."

There was silence between them for a moment. Then Mary gave a small chuckle as a memory came to her. "I remember when you were young and the first time you saw fireflies." She got a wistful look on her face. "You were so amazed at all the lights. I explained to you that it was just insects that were creating them, but you refused to believe it was something so mundane. You were convinced they were really little angels in disguise sent to brighten up the world. Every summer at twilight, you would run into the fields and catch a firefly to bring back and show me. Do you remember that?"

Sarah nodded, breathing deeply in a vain attempt to stop herself from becoming more upset. "Yes, I remember."

"I want you to make me a promise then." Mary took her daughter's hands in hers. "Promise me you will still try to find that amazement, whether it is with fireflies or endless summer days or whatever it may be, promise me that you will try to find happiness. The kind of happiness that makes you feel a childlike wonder. That makes you believe that there is still hope in this world. Promise me."

Sarah nodded her head as more tears threatened to fall from her eyes. "I promise," she whispered.

"Good, then I suppose this is farewell, my child." Mary turned her eyes down as they too began to fill with tears. When she looked back up, she pulled Sarah into a tight embrace. "Remember, I love you more than you will ever know."

"I love you too." Sarah's voice broke as she failed to stop her tears. "Thank you for everything. Thank you for being the most loving mother a child could ever want."

"No, 'tis I who should thank you for being a wonderful daughter." Mary now wept openly. "I know in the past I may have been wary of your fanciful nature, but I was wrong. Always be true to your inner heart. It is what makes you strong."

After several moments and more tender

exchanges, the two women pulled apart, both with reddened, wet faces. Mary reluctantly urged her daughter to go on her way and Sarah slowly went. Before leaving the room, she gave her mother one final nod. This injustice and the pain and sadness it caused were killing her inside. As she made her way outside of the prison, she slammed her back against the wall, sank to the ground, and wept.

❧

The family sat around the dinner table that night, a heavy gloominess among them. The fire was dying in the hearth, but no one cared to tend to it. Much of their dinner had gone uneaten and would be given to the animals the next day. Peter was the first to ask a question about the executions taking place the next day.

"What time tomorrow must we be there?" he asked.

"At the earliest, eight in the morning," John replied.

Ann meekly followed up Peter's question. "Where are they taking them anyway?"

"Some hill at the edge of Salem. The jailer gave me rough directions," her husband explained.

Ann nodded and the room fell silent again. Joseph suddenly broke the tenseness in the room by asking, "What about her body? We cannot leave her there."

"What do you propose?" John returned.

"We bring her here for burial, under cover of darkness," he replied.

John raised an eyebrow at him. "That is a great risk, you realize this?"

"It is a risk I am willing to take to give our mother the burial she deserves," he stated defiantly, knowing that no Christian burial was given to convicted witches.

His brother nodded. "Then tomorrow we shall have to arrange for it."

The room fell silent again until Peter sighed. "Well I am exhausted. Goodnight." He abruptly got up and left for bed.

Ann and Joseph soon followed him, leaving John and Sarah alone. Sarah stared at the candle before her, becoming transfixed on the flickering flame. She realized that she had no wish to see her mother's execution. It would be a gruesome event and she wanted no part of it.

"Must I go tomorrow?" she asked her brother quietly. "I do not want to see it."

"You must go," he insisted. "We must show her we support her."

"She knows we support her."

"It will mean more to her if she sees us all there," he explained. "Our presence will give her strength in her final moments. Do you want her to believe that in the end her own daughter abandoned her to face her fate alone?"

"How dare you?" Sarah stood up immediately from her seat. "I have not abandoned her. I would never do such a thing."

"Then tomorrow you will go with us to Salem," John stated firmly. He rose from the table and turned to go to bed, leaving Sarah alone with her thoughts.

She walked over to the window and saw the moon shining brightly in the distance. Leaning against the pane, she spoke quietly to the inanimate object.

"What would I give to be you right now?" She wanted to be removed from this pain; to be separated from this miserable situation.

She prayed one last time for a miracle before going to bed, "Dear God, please do not let her die. Please, I beg you to do something, anything to save her life." Of course, there was no reply to her prayer. As she stood in the quiet of the room, one thing became abundantly clear to her: tomorrow would be the worst day of her life.

❧

As night fell, Mary sat kneeling by the window in her cell, hands clasped in prayer. Only the moonlight provided any illumination in the darkness. The despair in Mary's soul was slowly giving way to bittersweet release. In a strange way, a part of her reasoned that perhaps it was best that her life would be ending. There would be no more suffering, no more worrying, no more sadness, only peace. Still, there was one thing that troubled her.

"God, I know you have deemed my time among the living to be over and so I will no longer be able to care for my children," she prayed. "Please guide them and protect them in my absence. Let no harm come to them. They are all that matter now."

Truly, the thought of her children and grandchildren hurt her the most. She wanted to see her youngest children marry and watch her grandchildren grow to be young adults. She wanted to see her family prosper well into the future and now she would be unable to. Praying some more, she also asked that no more trouble would come to them or anyone else.

"I know not why you have allowed this chaos to befall us, but please let it end," she continued. "I should like that no more of your loyal servants die unjustly."

She sat quietly thinking over her life. God had blessed her with a kind, industrious husband and many healthy, beautiful children. She never had to feel hunger or suffer from lack of shelter. Her life had not been as hard as others', but she could not bring herself to feel gratitude given what her present circumstances were. She had been given all of this, only for her life to be ripped away in such an unfortunate manner. Had she done something wrong in her past that warranted her fate now? Thinking back on her mistakes, she found nothing that she had not already repented for nor anything that seemed worthy of being executed for. She couldn't wrap her head around it. If she had committed a grievous sin, she could at least feel that she deserved her death.

Finally, she thought about her husband and the children she had lost. At least tomorrow they would all be reunited. "Nathan, I will see you soon," she whispered before crying silent tears once again.

CHAPTER NINE

September 22, 1692

An eerie silence had descended upon the Parker household that morning. There were hardly any words spoken among them. John came to Sarah's room to ensure that she was awake and readying herself for the day, much to her irritation. She did not appreciate him treating her as he would one of his children. Going through her clothes, she settled on her black dress as it was the only color to match her grim mood. She rubbed at her burning eyes, having gotten hardly any sleep the night before.

John arranged for one of their neighbors to watch his sons as none of them wanted young children to see such an abhorrent event. The family waited on the road for Elizabeth and Hannah to meet them. There was a chill in the air now as autumn began to set in and Sarah pulled her cloak tighter around her. Hannah was the first to arrive with her husband and Elizabeth and her husband followed soon after. Short greetings were exchanged between them before they proceeded on to Salem. The stillness among them continued on the way.

The place set for the executions was a rocky ledge located near the North River at the edge of Salem. At the top of the hill, eight nooses had already been arranged on some of the larger limbs protruding from one of the trees. The tree's gnarled branches stood in contrast to the pale gray sky above. It was an unwelcoming sight. There were already many other people waiting there. Some were family members of those about to die, while others were just looking for morbid entertainment. Several of the afflicted girls dared to show their faces and Sarah's anger was stoked once again upon seeing them.

After several more moments as they stood atop the hill waiting for the executions to begin, there was some commotion and many people started speaking at once. "What is happening?" Elizabeth asked, unable to see over the crowd with her shorter stature.

"It looks like the cart bringing the condemned up is stuck," Joseph replied.

"The devil hath halted it!" one of the afflicted girls cried out.

"He doth not want his servants to die!" another person shouted.

Sarah gritted her teeth and snarled, "Do they never stop?" They had already killed these people, could they not even spare them more slander in their final moments?

Finally, after much maneuvering, the sheriff and his men managed to bring the cart up to the top of the hill. There were seven women, including Mary, and one man, Samuel Wardwell, who was also from

Andover. His daughter had been one of Mary's accusers. Sarah wondered if her father's death was the girl's punishment for crying out against others. She looked at her mother, who seemed to be searching among the spectators for her family. Mary spotted Joseph first, his height allowing him to be seen more easily in the crowd, before looking at the rest of her children. Their solemn faces hurt her heart and she wanted to comfort them one last time, but could not.

One by one Sheriff Corwin and his men led the eight condemned down from the cart and to the nooses hanging from the tree. Each person was helped up a ladder where they were able to speak a few final words. Some of those present tried to get the condemned to confess one last time, but they all refused. The first person to be led up the ladder was Alice Parker of Salem, who was of no relation to the Parkers of Andover. When the ladder was removed from beneath her feet, she unfortunately did not die immediately. Instead, the victim thrashed about as her body struggled for breath and against the strangulating force of the rope. Horrified by the sight, Sarah turned her eyes down. She could only imagine what the others set to die must have been thinking now that they had to follow this gruesome example.

Two more women were hanged before Wardwell was brought up the ladder. He attempted to assert his innocence one last time. "Though the honorable jury has found me guilty, I have never used witchcraft to harm any person. I have..." He started to cough as the smoke from the executioner's tobacco pipe passed his face.

"The devil does not want him to speak!" a girl in the crowd exclaimed.

Wardwell ignored her and brokenly tried to continue. "I have only… ever committed my life to the Lord…and may God now welcome me into his kingdom above."

When his life was put to an end, the executioner moved onto the next woman. "Mary Esty, will you confess now?" one of the men in the crowd asked her.

"I will only confess to my innocence," she replied. "But I wish to bid farewell to my loving husband and my children and friends. They know of my piety and may they always know of my most sincere affection for them. All that I ask now is that no more innocent blood be shed."

Many people seemed to be deeply moved as the woman expressed her final thoughts. After she had been hanged, the executioner went over to Mary. Sarah's heartbeat quickened in anticipation as she felt Elizabeth's hand slide into her own. She gripped her sister's hand tight in response for support. Mary was led up the ladder and the noose was placed around her neck. For a brief moment, Sarah caught her mother's gaze. The expression in her eyes was unreadable and it would not be until years later that Sarah was able to put a name to it: acceptance. It was hard to understand how one could accept such a fate. Sarah would come to see that Mary was not so much accepting what had been done to her, but accepting that now was the end. At the end of the road lay peace. There was peace in death and knowing that the hardships of this world would be over. Perhaps her mother also took comfort in knowing that she would meet her God and be reunited with her deceased family members, or so she hoped. Regardless, she took her fate much more gracefully than most would have and Sarah came to admire her all the more for it.

"I wish to address my children," Mary said.

"You may," the sheriff's reply came.

"You know well of my enduring love for you, but do not mourn me," she spoke with her eyes fixed on her children. "Remember me with only fondness, for my death and that of the others shall now illuminate the grave mistakes made here this day. May our sacrifice be the salvation for those who have fallen to the devil's delusion... My sons and daughters, I love you all so much." Mary closed her eyes for a moment to keep the tears at bay. She inhaled deeply and spoke her final words. "And with that, I give my life to God." She gave a slight nod to Corwin to signal that she had finished and was ready to leave this world.

Sarah felt her throat become tight at her mother's painfully beautiful farewell. She couldn't help but feel pride at her mother's rebuking of the accusers. Her thoughts were broken as the executioner pulled away the ladder and her mother's body dropped forward. Sarah clenched her eyes shut, not wanting to see her mother's body dangling as it clung to life in her final moments. She soon found her hand pulling free from Elizabeth's and her feet pulling her away from the crowd to the edge of the cliff. Her tears were automatic and she grabbed onto one of the trees to prevent herself from falling over. A single drop from the ladder; that was all it took for her mother's life to end. Just like that, she was gone.

The last two women were summarily executed and the bodies were left hanging. Sarah did not want to look, but macabre curiosity got the better of her. She instantly regretted her decision. The vision of the eight bodies swaying gently around the tree and her mother's lifeless face slumped forward would forever be seared into her memory. For a moment, the only sound on the ledge was the wind sweeping through the trees. The silence was broken by the voice of Reverend Nicholas Noyes. "What a sad thing it is to see eight firebrands of hell hanging there," he announced as if his opinion was the most important in the world.

All of the members of the Parker family turned their heads toward him at once and gave him glares that could have frozen water in the middle of a summer heat wave. They were not alone as family members of others who were executed turned toward him as well. He even had the audacity to look pleased with his statement.

"No one asked for his declaration," John muttered

"He would do well to keep his ugly mouth shut," Joseph agreed.

After a long while, the crowd began to disperse and the officials began to cut the bodies down from the tree. Sarah's brothers continued to linger, watching the men move the bodies. It was not until the corpses had been laid in the dirt that they decided to leave. They were all quiet on the way home. When they arrived at the house, her brothers retreated to the barn while Ann went to fetch the children at the neighbor's house. Sarah wondered what her brothers were up to and quietly followed them. Keeping herself hidden from view, she tried hard to listen to them as best she could in their hushed tones.

"We must wait till dusk." She heard John's voice first. "We must not draw attention to ourselves."

"But we cannot leave too late or we will not be able to see the way," Peter countered.

"Then I suppose we will just have to hurry," Joseph's voice came next. "In the meantime, I will set to digging."

Sarah heard the scrape of metal before Joseph emerged from the barn with a shovel. He stopped short in surprise when he saw her standing there with her arms folded over her chest and annoyance gracing her face.

"So have you indeed decided to retrieve our mother's body?" she asked.

"Eavesdropping now, are you?" he replied. "And yes, we have."

"I do not appreciate secrets involving her being kept from me," she growled.

John and Peter soon emerged from the barn, having heard their sister's complaint. "We meant to keep no secrets from you," John explained. "But there is no need for you to be involved. We will handle it."

"She is my mother too, I should be involved," she spat. "I thought you would understand that given how just last night you were lecturing me about abandoning her."

Peter and Joseph looked confused, but John set his mouth to a firm line. "Sarah, it is better if you remain at home," he said.

"This seems to be a task where you will need all the help you can receive," she retorted. "I will be going with you." And with that, she turned from them sharply.

"One moment she wishes not to go to Salem, the next she is determined to walk her way there if she must. Does she always have to be so damned stubborn?" John grumbled to his brothers.

"But she would not be our sister then, would she? God help the man who takes her as a wife," Joseph said before he proceeded to the spot where they had planned for their mother's grave.

The planned burial site was to be near the great oak tree as they believed that would be a fitting resting place for their mother. Joseph set to work digging while his brothers were busy attempting to fashion a rough coffin. He soon found another shovel joining his and looked up to see his sister.

"Sarah, what are you doing?" he asked in exasperation and stopped his work.

"Helping," she stated firmly without ceasing her movements. "It will take too long if you do it by yourself."

"You should not be doing this, leave it to me."

"I am capable of shoveling dirt," she yelled at him, then spoke softer. "And besides, I need something to distract my mind."

That seemed to make him silent for the time being and he continued his work. Sarah had only gotten about six inches down on the area she was working with when she hit something with her shovel. She stooped down to brush some of the dirt aside with her hand. A bottle soon appeared buried upside down in the earth and she carefully removed it from the soil. It was a corked bottle made of green glass and there was something moving around inside it. Holding it up to the light, she could see what appeared to be nails and some sort of liquid inside it.

"What is this supposed to be?" she asked turning to her brother, although she feared she already had an idea.

He took the bottle from her and held it up to the light as well, examining it. "I think I know what this is," he stated. "Some people believe if you take a bottle and fill it with nails, pins, and even urine, and bury it upside down in the ground, it will remove whatever affliction a witch has put on you."

"But why is there one here?" she asked. "You do not suppose Mother or Father did it?"

"I cannot say," he said. "I have never known anyone in this household to submit to such practices nor to have been harmed by a witch. Perhaps John would know better than I."

He put the bottle aside and continued to dig. Sarah resumed her work, but could not stop thinking of the bottle. It gave her a strange feeling of dread that she could not shake, like she had unearthed something she should not have. The idea that someone within their household may possibly have resorted to using countercharms unnerved her. The siblings dug as much as they could before exhaustion set in. Soon the sun began to recede over the horizon and they would have to begin their journey to Salem.

John and Joseph hitched the horses to a cart and Sarah brought a lantern and sheet to cover her mother's body with. Peter had placed two shovels in the cart, not quite sure of how much dirt they needed to move. Luckily, there was hardly anyone out of doors on the road this late in the day. As they approached Salem, it became harder to see in the dim light and the sky filled with clouds threatening a storm. The siblings had decided to travel through the edge of the woods to prevent themselves from being seen as much as possible. As they got nearer to the place of the executions, Sarah grabbed John's hand in panic and stopped him from pulling the horses further.

"Sarah, what are you doing?" he yelled at her.

"Shhh, look." She nodded her head toward two men on horseback coming near them. They appeared to be men of some sort of authority, out patrolling the town.

John carefully urged the horses to move deeper into the woods and out of sight of the men, pulling the cart behind a cluster of trees. Sarah hid the lantern under her cloak to conceal its light. The family waited with bated breath as the men came nearer to them. A snap from somewhere in the forest resounded and all four of them jumped in fright. The noise caught the men's attention and they stopped for a moment, looking out into the woods. One of the men brought his horse closer to the trees and tried looking for whatever it was that made the sound. Out of nowhere, a deer ran from the trees and in front of the men. The horse of the man nearest to the trees bucked up in fright and the man worked quickly to calm the spooked animal. The deer continued in the other direction toward the trees on the opposite side of the path.

"Damn deer!" the man growled. "I should hunt the beast and make good on supper with it."

"Aye, I have not had venison for some time," the other replied and the two men brought their horses to a trot and continued on.

The Parkers all breathed with relief and continued on their way as well. Eventually, after what seemed an eternity, they reached the ledge. Peter and Joseph tied the horses to one of the trees and the family carefully scaled the cliff. Sarah walked by John to light the way. He was trying to remember the exact location of where he had seen the officials place their mother's body, but everything seemed different in the dark. Finally, he came to a spot that sat low on the ledge.

"Here, I think this is where they were buried," he stated.

As Sarah shone the light over the ground, several fresh large mounds of dirt appeared. She swallowed hard. What they were doing filled her with sadness and shame at the same time. Disturbing the dead in the dark felt unholy, but she had to remind herself that her mother was not given an appropriate burial. The shallow grave she had been placed in was undignified for such a pious, kind-hearted woman who was innocent of the crime she was convicted of. She deserved a proper Christian burial and that was what they were here to accomplish.

"Do you know exactly which grave is hers?" Joseph asked.

"Well, it was not that one." Peter pointed at one of the graves that had already been dug up.

"Looks like someone else had the same idea," John said quietly as he moved toward the graves in the middle of the burial.

He took one of the shovels and carefully started to remove the dirt from one of the graves. Strange anticipation filled them as they waited for the head of a corpse to appear. When one finally did, Sarah brought the lantern closer to it. John brushed the dirt from the face to get a better look at its features. The face was that of a woman, but not their mother's. John moved on to the next mound and Joseph took a shovel and began to do the same.

Sarah heard a rustling coming from behind them and she turned around swiftly. Holding the lantern up, she looked around the ledge to see what had made the noise. She was not sure what would have scared her more, one of the sheriff's men or the spirit of one of the executed. The lantern barely lit the landscape past a few yards, but the areas it did shine through only created shadows in the form of the twisting trees.

"Sarah!" Joseph's harsh voice brought her out of her fright. "Bring the lantern over here!"

"Sorry, I thought I heard something," she explained but did as he instructed.

"Never mind that now," he scolded her as she held the light up over the body he had unearthed. They both examined it. "Not her." He shook his head.

"I think I have found her," John's voice came to them, quiet and somber.

Sarah brought the lantern over to where he was and shone the light upon the corpse. Sure enough, the pale, gray face of Mary appeared. Sarah felt tears come to her eyes as she looked upon the body of her mother, covered in dirt and bugs. Joseph began to help his brother dig out the rest of the grave. When her whole body was visible, John and Joseph handed the shovels to Sarah while they and Peter worked to lift up the cold, stiff body. Maneuvering both shovels and the lantern, Sarah followed her brothers carefully down the side of the cliff and to the cart.

They had just placed their mother's body in the cart when they heard the sound of horses trotting toward them. They all froze as a group of people came into view. The group consisted of four men, the youngest of whom appeared to be barely Peter's age. They stared at the Parkers, who stared back at them, an awkward silence filling the air between them as neither group was sure what to say to the other. Eventually, one of the older men in the other group looked into the cart, staring at Mary's body.

"We have come for our dead also," he said, turning back to the Parkers.

"Up the hill to your right, you will find several graves between a small tree and one of the larger rocks," John said. "Forgive us if we disturbed the burial of your relative, but we could not find our mother's so easily."

"Nothing to forgive," the man replied before turning to the others with, "We best be getting to work before the rain sets in."

He nodded at John before he and the others with him began to climb the ledge. Sarah turned to look up at the night sky and felt soft droplets of rain on her face. Joseph took the shovels from her and put them in the cart before Peter and John laid the blanket over their mother. They all climbed up into the cart and began the ride back to Andover. A crack of thunder shattered the quiet of the night and the rain started to come down harder. They prayed they would not get caught in the mud or that the roads would become impossible to transverse.

It was difficult to both keep an eye out for officials and to see through the dark and the rain. While they were all anxious about returning home without any problems, Sarah was feeling even more nervous than her brothers. She kept looking around constantly, any little noise frightening her. For some reason, she kept feeling as though they were being followed, and she wasn't entirely sure it was by another human. Riding through the path in the woods was not helping matters. The twisted branches and thick swathes of leaves concealed what might be hiding in the woods and she feared any moment something would jump out at them.

John was urging the horses on faster now, trying to get home before the rain became heavier. The trees zipped by as they rode, but something caught Sarah's eye in the darkness. Something white was up ahead by the trees. As they came closer, the shape of a woman dressed all in white became apparent and Sarah felt her blood run cold. The woman seemed to not even notice them, walking with a slow, uneven gait and keeping her head turned down. Sarah could not take her eyes from the woman and even turned around to stare at her as they passed. When the woman was finally out of sight, she turned back to see if her brothers had noticed her.

"Did you see that woman?" she asked.

"What woman?" Peter turned around and looked at the receding trees.

"There was a woman in white walking in the forest," she replied.

"I saw no woman," he said.

Joseph and John also agreed that they hadn't seen a woman walking through the trees. *A spirit she was then,* Sarah thought to herself as a chill ran through her body. She pulled the hood of her cloak tighter over her head, hoping it would conceal her from any more wandering souls as well as the rain. She looked down for much of the remainder of the ride home, not wanting to see anything else supernatural in appearance.

After successfully navigating the treacherous muddy roads, they arrived at their home. A light could still be seen in one of the rooms on the first floor. Ann must have stayed up waiting for them to return and her face soon became visible as she looked out the window upon hearing the horses and cart. John waved to her before continuing on to the barn. It was needless for any of them to say that a burial would not be occurring tonight with the rain. Entering the barn, they found themselves soaked to the bone and shivering in the chilly September night.

"Leave her in the cart for the night," John stated as he began to unhitch the horses. "Tomorrow we will bury her."

They nodded in agreement but said nothing else. As her brothers went to tend to the horses, Sarah walked back over to the cart. Gently and with great dread, she lifted the blanket away from her mother's face. A deathly pallor had set in with the skin now pale and in stark contrast to the dirt still covering her cheeks and forehead. Her eyelids had opened slightly, revealing the lifeless eyes beneath them. Seeing the light now gone from Mary's eyes, the finality of her death hit Sarah hard and she began to cry. She looked down and saw the noose still around Mary's neck. Pulling the shroud down further, she saw her wrists were still bound in rope as well.

Looking around through her tears, she spotted a knife on the worktable. She set to work cutting away at the ropes, finding the task harder than normal in her despair. When her mother was finally free of the bindings, Sarah set the knife back down on the table and looked back at her mother before going inside for the night. With gentle fingers, she caressed her mother's cold cheek and pressed her eyelids closed. A tear drop fell on Mary's forehead as Sarah whispered how sorry she was and how much she loved her. Slowly, she pulled the blanket back up over her mother's body and took one last glance at her before closing the barn door.

Once back in the house, Sarah waited until she was alone before turning her attention to the fireplace. She took the remnants of the noose and wrist bindings and threw them in the fire. A loud thunderclap sounded as she did so, but Sarah paid it no mind. She was too focused on watching the tools used in her mother's execution burn. *It was no execution,* the voice in her head stated, *they murdered her.* And with an unsettling mixture of sadness, anger, and hopelessness, she watched the ropes turn to ash as flames reflected in her eyes.

❧

The rain continued to come down in sheets that night with the occasional accompaniment of thunder and lightning. Between crying and the loud thunder, Sarah was unable to find sleep. Eventually, she dragged herself out of bed and over to the window. Looking outside, she could hardly see anything in the pitch black. Then suddenly, lightning struck and illuminated the landscape briefly. Her eyes turned toward the oak in the yard where she could have sworn she saw something out of place. She waited until the lightning struck again and then she saw a figure standing by the oak tree. A gasp escaped her lips and she stumbled back in fright, yet she could not tear her eyes away from the tree. The next time lightning struck, there was no one there. Her heart beat wildly and her mind clouded with fear. She quickly hurried back to bed and under the covers. As her heart stilled and her breathing returned to normal, she tried to reason with herself that it was just her mind playing tricks on her due to her tiredness and grief. Yet, she could not help feeling that it was something else entirely.

◌𝕾

The next morning was a surreal experience for Sarah. When she awoke, she kept expecting to see her mother downstairs in the kitchen. It didn't seem real that she was dead and it seemed even less real that she died in such a manner as she had. Sarah kept questioning if the events of the last month had actually happened. Someone being executed for witchcraft was something that happened to other people, something that one would hear about secondhand in the form of local gossip, but for it to happen to a member of her own family... it just seemed impossible. She was ever hopeful that she would wake up from a horrific nightmare.

The rain from last night had ceased, but the ground was still muddy. It made digging out a grave easier, but the soil heavier. Regardless, the family persevered to give their mother a proper burial. John and Joseph had laid the body in the makeshift coffin. Sarah made her way into the barn and saw that the corpse was showing further signs of decay. Still, she did her best to clean off her mother's face and brush as much of the dirt from her clothes as possible. She got the idea in her head to snip off a lock of her mother's hair. With some careful maneuvering, she managed the task. Holding the lock in her hand, Sarah realized that they had the same hair color and it made her sad to think that people were probably right when they said she looked the most like her mother out of all of her siblings.

Apparently, her brothers had informed Hannah and Elizabeth of their plans and waited for them to come with their husbands and children. When they finally did, the family members took turns paying their respects to Mary. When Sarah was alone with her once again, she broke down. Unbearable guilt wove its way around her and refused to let go. "Mama, I am sorry, so sorry," she cried, "I am sorry I could not save you. I should have done something, anything. I should have tried harder." A lot of what she spoke she had already said last night, but she repeated it anyway as if to affirm it not only to Mary's spirit but to herself. "You had too great a heart for this. You should not have died in this way. God could not have granted me a better mother." Her crying became furious and her words came out broken. "I love you so much." She bent and kissed Mary's forehead, then whispered, "Goodbye."

Her brothers went into the barn again and nailed the coffin shut. With the help of their in-laws, the five men worked together to place the coffin in the grave. John and Joseph spoke a few words before leading the group in prayer, but Sarah didn't feel like praying and remained silent. How hard had she prayed before her mother's execution for her to be spared? All of it came to naught and, as far as she was concerned, there was no sense in praying now.

After the service, the men set to work shoveling

dirt back into the grave and the women went back to the house. Ann carried her youngest son in her arms while the older one walked by her side. "So will I really never see Grandmother again?" Jacob looked up at his mother with sorrowful eyes.

Ann shook her head softly at him. "One day, in heaven perhaps you will, but not while you walk among the living."

The little boy turned from her, keeping his eyes to the ground. Sarah pitied the child as he came to terms with his first brush with death and tried to understand it. As they made their way inside, the women and children all gathered around the table in the main room. Instead of joining them, Sarah went upstairs to her room and shut herself inside. She didn't want to be around anyone. She did not want to listen to any idle chatter or bittersweet remembrances of her mother. What she really wanted was for time to reverse itself so that she could have told her family to leave this province turned hell on earth before it was too late or perhaps to break her mother out of prison and help her run away. She would give anything for her mother to still be alive.

CHAPTER TEN

In the days following Mary's execution, the family spent their time mourning their mother and trying to adjust to life without her. It was strange not seeing her about the house anymore or being able to go to speak to her, given that she had been such a mainstay in their lives. They found it hard to speak about her as well, only occasionally bringing up some past memory they had of her. Even their moods had changed drastically. John was harsher than usual, Joseph no longer made light of anything, Peter had taken to being sullen all the time, and Sarah stopped her hopeful daydreaming and became more irritable. She even began to lose interest in the things that used to make her happy and it took all her energy to get her to do her daily chores.

Sarah would often find herself crying about her mother and once again repeating how sorry she was. She sometimes opened up to Joseph on these occasions, but he too felt guilty about not doing more to save Mary. Despite their guilt, he tried to rationalize for both of them that any attempts they may have made would have come to nothing. Mary's life was forfeit from the start as the entire judicial system was broken. Still, it did nothing to make Sarah feel better.

One night in particular, she found herself tossing and turning. Her mind was racing with all sorts of negative thoughts as the events of the last few weeks replayed in her head. Sighing, she got up from her bed and decided to walk around for a bit. That sometimes helped her on nights like these. She noticed that the fire in her hearth was being fueled by the last piece of wood in the room. Getting some more firewood from downstairs would give her an excuse to be up and walking about should anyone question why she was not in bed. Taking a candle with her, she made her way downstairs. The main room of the house was eerily quiet. There was not even the sound of wind or animals from outside that could be heard in the room. The candle's flame bathed the room in dull light and cast unsettling shadows on the walls. The dark corners of the room that the candle's light did not reach gave Sarah an uneasy feeling. She felt as if she were not alone and that someone was watching her.

With firewood in hand, she hurried up the stairs. Upon entering the upstairs hallway, she heard light thumping noises coming from her mother's bedroom. Her heart started to beat faster in her chest as she approached the door. She opened it slowly and hesitantly moved the candle into the room. The candlelight did not reach far, but nothing seemed to be out of the ordinary. Then softly from the dark recesses of the room came a whisper. It was unintelligible, but unmistakable in being a human voice… a female voice.

Sarah, in a fright, slammed the door and ran with unnatural speed back to her own room. She hurried inside and closed the door behind her. Clumsily, she dropped the firewood by the hearth before jumping into bed and pulling the covers over her head. If the panic she felt had not been so real, the scene might have been comical. Her behavior was like that of a five-year-old, not a grown woman. Her heart was beating so loudly she could hear it in the quiet of her room and could feel her pulse through her skin. She was desperately trying not to breathe loudly but found her breathing labored under the blankets. Carefully, she peeked her head out from beneath the covers to allow herself to breathe easier. Still, she was on alert as her body became rigid and she tried not to make a sound as she listened in the darkness.

After what seemed like an eternity, she began to calm down. She had to remind herself to breathe deeply so that her heart rate could return to normal. What was that? Who was in that room? Was it her mother's ghost? The questions filled her frantic mind. Whatever it was, she refused to leave the safety of her bed and she prayed that the sun would come up soon.

The next morning, John was waiting for her by the downstairs fireplace. "Can you explain to me what all of that noise was last night?" he asked. He was staring at her accusingly. He had dark circles under his eyes, indicating that he too had trouble sleeping and Sarah's antics hadn't helped matters.

"I… I was unable to sleep. I went downstairs to retrieve some firewood for my fireplace. I was going back to my room when I heard noises coming from

Mother's room." She paused for a moment, finding it hard to continue. "I heard a whisper inside the room. I was so terrified I slammed the door and ran back to my room."

"So you disturbed my sleep because you are going mad." John's voice was full of irritation.

"I am not going mad," Sarah defended herself, voice raising in the process, "I heard something. I swear it."

"You are exhausted and full of grief," he replied as he turned back to the fire, then said quietly, "We all are. The mind can be unreliable at such times."

Something in his tone made Sarah stop. "Something has happened to you as well?" It was more a statement than a question. He gave Sarah a sideways glance but said nothing. "Tell me," she urged him.

He sighed before answering her. "When I was bringing in the last of the harvest yesterday, I… I thought I saw a figure from the corner of my eye," he said softly. "When I turned, however, there was no one there."

They were both silent for several moments. Sarah gently walked over to the table and sat down. She breathed deeply before saying, "She lingers still. I can feel it. She has not left us."

"You cannot speak of ghosts," John said. "Mother is gone. We must leave her to rest now."

"For her sake or ours?" Sarah could not help but feel hurt at his dismissive attitude.

"Both." His answer was firm. "We must leave the dead to eternal peace and we cannot fill ourselves with this false hope or whatever it may be."

"I wish I could let her go as easily as you," she

said icily. He glared at her before leaving the room. She sighed and sank back into the chair.

⚭

Six days had passed since their mother's execution and Sarah's grief turned into quietly boiling rage. She was filled with anger at how unjust her mother's death had been and she was frustrated at not being able to reverse it. How she wished that she could tear down the entire judicial system and make everyone, from the magistrates to the accusers, pay for what they did to her mother and the other families they had torn apart.

She now sat quietly on her bed lost in these thoughts. Only the sound of the fire crackling in the hearth and the wind blowing against the windowpane interrupted the silence. The stillness in the room was broken when the door burst open. Peter rushed into the room looking thoroughly panicked. He pulled at her arm trying to get her up from her bed.

She pulled back against him. "Peter, what are you doing?" she asked in alarm.

"They have come for you!" he cried. "You must run!"

"What? Not again." The color drained from her face.

"Please, you need to leave before they can take you." He tugged at her arm again trying to get her to move.

Her body finally caught up with her brain and she jumped up from the bed. The two made for the stairs, with Peter telling her to go out the back door. "But where shall I go?" she asked frantically.

"Somewhere, anywhere but here!" he exclaimed as he dashed down the stairs.

They finally reached the bottom of the stairs where they saw John and Joseph at the front door blocking Constable Ballard from entering the house. Her heart racing, Sarah quickly decided that if she could make it to the barn and hide in the loft or behind some of the equipment until he left, that would spare her some time to think of what to do next. Making her way to the back door, she looked around before running to the barn. She had only made it a few yards when she was suddenly pulled forcefully back. She screamed as a pair of arms wound their way around her body and she struggled to free herself.

"I have her!" the man who held her called out.

Ballard came running around from the front of the house with her brothers in tow. "Figured you would give me trouble," he said as he approached Sarah, still struggling in the other man's arms. "Glad I brought help."

He went to bind Sarah's hands but she kicked out at him and hit him in the lower stomach. He cried out, but instead of harming him she only made him angrier and more determined. The man holding her turned to the side so that she would not be able to kick at Ballard again. Ballard reached for her arms, but she writhed away from him and kept trying to arch her back to break free of the man holding her. Joseph grabbed at Ballard, but the man threw his arm back and hit Joseph in the face, knocking him to the ground. There was a shout behind her and she was knocked free from the other man's arms. Turning, she saw that Peter had jumped on the other man's back and was fighting with him. She tried to take off running again, but Ballard grabbed her and managed to pin her down in order to bind her wrists. Despite her struggle, she once again was on her way to Salem.

છ

Sarah practically made Ballard and the other man drag her into the courtroom. If they wanted to condemn her, she was going to make them work for it. She stood at the edge of the room with both men on either side of her. The magistrates had just finished examining one of the accused who was now being led out.

"Sarah Parker," one of the judges announced her name. "Come forward."

She felt anxiety grow within her, but she refused to move. The men, however, saw to that and pulled her forward and she fought against their grip the entire time. She was certain she would have bruises by the time this was over. They forcibly sat her down in the chair before the magistrates. Several of the afflicted girls were there and they immediately began writhing in place upon seeing Sarah. She noticed the Phelps girl was once again among the accusers. A dangerous thought came into Sarah's head then. She wished she truly were a witch so that she could beat them all to silence without hindrance.

Her thoughts were broken by the voice of one of the magistrates, who stated, "You are accused of afflicting Sarah Phelps. How long have you been in league with the devil?"

"I know nothing of it. I do not covenant with him!" she spat back at him.

The afflicted girls began to fall ever deeper into their convulsions with their bodies contorting this way and that. Some began to cry out in pain.

"Will you not recover them from their fits?" the judge asked.

She snarled her reply. "If they wish to be recovered from their fits, they have it well within their means to do so for themselves."

"Do you mean they pretend?" He cocked an eyebrow at her.

"'Tis exactly what they do."

"But how can you lack heart enough to say so? Look at the pains you bring them." He gestured to the girls.

"How can one so learned be so naïve as to fall victim to the whims of distracted persons?" she asked snidely.

"You will recover them now!" he commanded.

Sarah remained where she was, however, and only responded with a firm, "No."

"Then you will be forced to." He gestured to two guards.

Sarah once again felt herself being grabbed and dragged over to where the accusers had fallen. Her hand was forced forward and she touched each of the four girls who were twisting their bodies around. As expected, each girl ceased her fits and Sarah was led back to her place before the judges.

"Elizabeth Johnson, also of Andover, claims you joined with her and her sister Abigail Faulkner in afflicting Sarah Phelps and three of the Martin children." The magistrate looked down at the papers before him as he spoke. "How do you answer this charge?"

"Elizabeth Johnson is too ignorant of mind to know what she says." Sarah felt her blood starting to boil and she was shaking with anger.

"The widow Johnson's character is not in question at this time." Now it was Judge Hathorne who reprimanded her. "Please answer to whether you afflicted the aforesaid persons or not."

"I. Did. Not." She pronounced each word sharply through clenched teeth.

"But Sarah Phelps claimed that you were at her bedside two nights ago and pinched and pricked her," he informed her.

"Well, it would not be the first time that she spoke falsely." Sarah thought back to the girl's claims against her mother.

"You claim her to be a liar?" He looked at her like she was insane.

"I know not what else to call her."

Hathorne shook his head at her in disapproval. "'Tis shameful that you are unsympathetic to her pains."

"And it is not only they who know you to be in the snare of the devil," another magistrate continued where Hathorne left off. "You were named by Rebecca Eames. She stated that she did not know you to be a witch, but that you had been crossed in love and that the devil came to you and kissed you."

"What absurdity is this?" Sarah was taken aback by such a strange claim. "It is a ridiculous statement and a lie. Surely my lips would be burned from my body were it true."

The third judge continued, "Further, Susannah Post claims you were one of several people who attended a meeting of witches in Andover. What do you say to this claim?"

"I am not aware of any meeting of witches," she answered. "There were several people at this meeting you say?"

"Yes, Mistress Post approximated that there were two hundred witches in attendance."

"Two hundred!" Sarah exclaimed in false alarm. She then continued in a sarcastic tone, "I wonder how is it that a meeting so large could go unnoticed by everyone else in the town? I fear that your honors are not doing your duty of protecting the good people of this province if you are allowing the servants of the devil to meet in this large a size."

"Do you dare mock us, girl?" Hathorne asked sharply.

"As if I could resist such an opportunity when given it." Sarah smirked, knowing she had riled up the judges. Several snickers arose from the gathered onlookers.

"Enough!" Hathorne's voice boomed and the crowd fell silent at once. "You will show respect to this court." His eyes narrowed at Sarah and her eyes in turn challenged him.

"I will show respect when these proceedings deem worthy of it." Her tone was cold, all humor gone from it.

"You would do well to cease with these snide remarks," he reprimanded her as she simply shrugged her shoulders and sighed. "What? Do you have more to say?"

"You are going to imprison me anyway as you already presume my guilt. Why did you even bother bringing me before you?"

"If that is how you feel about it, take her," he

commanded as he turned to the guards.

They roughly grabbed Sarah by the arms and escorted her out of the courtroom. She managed to catch sight of her family before they took her out. Most of them gave her sympathetic looks, but John wore an expression Sarah could not quite put a name to. It seemed a cross between irritation and disappointment and it left Sarah with an odd feeling of embarrassment.

CB

"Should have known we would still not be safe," Sarah said in resignation, as she was led into Salem prison's common room.

"Well, making a mockery of the court certainly was of no help," John said as her brothers followed her.

"It matters not what I said," venom pouring into her words. "After what they have done to our mother, did you really expect me to show them any respect when they deserve none?"

"Of course not, but you may have expedited your own condemnation," John reminded her.

"They will kill me regardless of what I say. I thought they had made that quite clear," she scoffed.

"I cannot believe this is happening again," he sighed and rubbed his face tiredly.

"Of course it is happening; as if these people would give us any relief. Even when Mother and the others were executed they still could not stop spewing lies." Sarah became disgusted thinking of the accusations hurled on that day.

"They should hang for it!" Joseph growled. When

Sarah turned toward him, the look in his eyes startled her. He looked angry like she had never seen him and she could feel the hatred radiating from him. Joseph may not have taken a lot of things seriously, but when it came to protecting his family he was fearsome.

"Be still, brother." John laid a hand on his shoulder to try and calm him.

But Joseph violently shook his hand off. "No! Are we going to let them murder our entire family?" he roared.

"Joseph, please lower your voice," John hissed. They were all startled by their brother's outburst.

"Let them hear me! Let them know how they have torn our lives apart!" he continued to shout.

The jailer, who had heard Joseph's yelling, called out, "Hey! You keep it down over there or out you go!"

"Then go ahead and throw me out!" Joseph was undeterred.

"Joseph, please stop," Sarah begged him, grabbing onto his arm. "Believe me, no one is angrier than I to find ourselves in this predicament again, but you will be of more support to me if you are calm." He looked into her pleading eyes and felt his shoulders relax. He took a deep breath just as the jailer came over.

"Do we have a problem here, boy?" he grumbled.

Joseph glared at him, but John came to his aide. "Forgive my brother," he stated. "We have had a trying time of late."

"Keep him in line or he will not be allowed in here anymore," the jailer ordered as he shot one last look at Joseph.

"As if I want to be here anyway," Joseph grumbled as the other man walked away.

"At least you are not the one who has to be locked away in here," Sarah said, her voice breaking. She felt herself on the verge of tears. "I do not want to stay here."

Peter suddenly wrapped his arms around her. "We do not want you to be here either," he said quietly.

She returned his embrace and broke down, crying into his shoulder. "We will come to see you often," she heard Joseph's voice behind her and his hand on her back.

She nodded and slowly pulled away from Peter. Wiping her eyes with her sleeve, she tried to compose herself. "Do not burden yourselves," she told them. "I know the ride is long from home."

"Still we shall come whenever possible," John responded.

With that, she bid her brothers farewell and was taken to a cell after they left. As she entered the cell, all eyes turned upon her. The prisoners looked to see who would be joining them now. She was startled at how they stared at her, but they soon turned away uninterested. Sarah released the breath she did not realize she had been holding as the jailer chained her wrists. It felt like a block of ice had dropped into her stomach when she heard the clicking of the metal. Suddenly, her loss of freedom became all too real.

She stood for a moment taking in her surroundings before she heard a voice from behind her. "Are you one of them?"

She turned to see a woman, perhaps in her late twenties or early thirties, looking up at her. Her unkempt bright red hair was falling out from beneath her cap and her emerald eyes shone with curiosity. Sarah also noticed the woman wasn't wearing shackles.

"Am I one of what?" Sarah asked, turning toward her.

"One of the witches?" she inquired again.

"'Tis what they *claim* I am," she responded bitterly.

"So you are another innocent then," she stated, her expression full of mirth. "I must be the only guilty person in this entire jail."

"Are you admitting to being a witch then?" Sarah walked toward her.

"Oh no dear, I am not guilty of that," she said calmly. "I find myself imprisoned now for the much simpler crime of fornication… and striking my former lover when he confessed to it."

Sarah balked at the woman's nonchalance, as if being imprisoned for such a crime was apart of one's daily routine. She remembered all too well how ashamed her family had been when Hannah had gotten in trouble for fornication before her marriage. This woman seemed to think nothing of it. As she studied the woman, Sarah could tell that she used her more than generous figure and beautiful face to allure men. Yet, imprisonment for fornication was not something often heard of.

"Come sit." The woman patted the straw next to her. "Not much else to do, I fear." As Sarah sat next to her, the woman extended her hand. "The name is Martha."

"Mine is Sarah," she replied as she took the other woman's hand. "Why were you imprisoned for fornication? I thought such a crime warranted a fine only."

"I was fined the first time, then whipped the

second," Martha explained. "I suppose when I had not learned my lesson by the third offense, they thought a three-day stay in prison would correct my poor behavior. It has been well since three days' time, however."

"Then why are you still here?" Sarah knitted her eyebrows in confusion.

"My family refuses to pay my jail fees," she replied and Sarah could hear the bitterness in her voice. "They have decided to inflict their own punishment upon me for being a constant nuisance to them."

"Being whipped would have been a lesser punishment," Sarah quipped.

"I would certainly have preferred it," Martha muttered.

Sarah said nothing more and instead took in her surroundings. The cell was small and there were three other women besides her and Martha. It seemed the five of them would barely have room to sleep if they lay completely stretched out. Sarah tried to observe their faces without seeming too intrusive. She did not recognize any of them as people she knew. One was a woman who looked to be in her fifties and looked so frail and forlorn that Sarah wondered if she might die before the court would pass sentence upon her. Another was a woman who looked to be in her early forties and she sat rocking back and forth, staring at the wall. The last sat next to the rocking woman. She was a woman younger than Sarah and based upon her features, Sarah wondered if she and the rocking woman were related. The teen looked incredibly distraught as well.

Dear God, this is what this place will do to me. The

thought arose in Sarah's mind. She subconsciously curled her body inward as panic suddenly rose in her mind. She was stuck here and she couldn't leave. She would have to sit here night and day in these heavy chains, slowly losing her mind for a crime she was not guilty of. No longer could she do as she pleased or go where she wanted. She would be forced to suffer in this dark, cold cell with strangers for God only knows how long. *Trapped, they have me trapped. I am alone in this hellhole without any freedom,* her thoughts rambled on.

Her breathing suddenly became rapid as anxiety built within her and she found it hard to breathe. She felt pain in her chest and her heart started beating rapidly. She grew more afraid as the pain increased. "Oh God, oh no, no, no, no," she whispered.

"What is wrong?" Martha became startled at Sarah's sudden distress.

"My… my chest," she tried to get out.

"Oh dear Lord," Martha gasped. "Breathe deeply, please. Try to calm down." She kneeled beside Sarah and started to rub soothing circles on her back.

Sarah felt her skin starting to get sweaty and her vision blurred. Her fingers started to feel numb and she tried to clench and unclench her hands. "My hands…" She trailed off.

Martha grabbed both sides of her face and said firmly, "Look at me." Sarah blinked rapidly as she tried to pick her head up and focus on Martha's face. "Come now, take deep breaths."

Sarah tried to do as she was told, but it was doing nothing to assuage her fear. She tried to shake her head, hoping Martha would understand her meaning.

"Is she all right?" another woman in the cell asked.

"She will be fine," Martha answered.

"No, I am dying…" Sarah whispered.

"No, no, you are not dying," the older woman reasoned with her. "How old are you?" Sarah was confused about why she would suddenly ask that, but Martha urged her on. "Tell me, how old are you?"

"Twenty-two," Sarah managed to mumble.

"Good." Martha nodded. "What is your last name?"

"Parker." Sarah shook her head. "Why… why are you asking me these questions?"

"So you will focus on something else," the woman answered before continuing, "Now where are you from?"

"Andover."

"And how many siblings do you have?"

"Five, living."

As Martha continued to question her, she started to feel herself calming down. The pain in her chest subsided and her breathing returned to normal. "There, good girl," Martha stated, patting her back.

"How… how did you know to do that?" Sarah was stunned at the woman's apparent healing abilities.

"Do you think you are the first person I have seen working themselves up into a frenzy?" She gave Sarah a comforting smile. "What scared you so?"

"That I am stuck in here," Sarah answered. "I cannot bear to stay here."

"While I agree this prison is most unpleasant, I fear you will in turn become used to it," Martha said matter-of-factly.

"And if I cannot?" Sarah was afraid to hear her answer. "Then mad you will become."

CHAPTER ELEVEN

Samuel walked up the road that wound through Andover with a bounce in his step. He was finally home and breathed in relief and contentment upon seeing the welcoming sight of his house in the distance. A bullet had shot through his left arm during a brush he and the other men had with some of the locals, leaving him too injured to continue his service. He was sent home with the arm wrapped in a sling so that he would not move it unnecessarily. Samuel increased his speed as he came nearer to the house, wanting to get home as fast as possible. He had not even gotten within ten yards of it when the front door flew open and his mother came running out.

"Samuel!" she cried and threw her arms around him.

"Mother, 'tis good to be home with you once again, but I should not like my arm to be injured more," he grunted as her embrace pushed into his damaged left arm.

"Forgive me," she said as she hurriedly pulled back. "But you know not the worry you have put me through in these last few months."

"Then it is I who should apologize to you." He smiled at her as they walked back to the house together.

"Oh, how I missed you," she said endearingly. She looked at his left arm and asked, "Has your arm improved at all since you last wrote?"

"It hurts a bit less now," he replied. "The physician says I must move it once it heals more or the joint will stiffen."

"When was the last time the bandages were changed?" she asked.

"I think maybe two days ago," he stated.

"I should change them again then," she told him with a gentle smile.

At the front door, his father and brother were waiting for him. "Ah, Sam finally come home to us," his father announced as he put an arm around his son.

Samuel returned his embrace with his good arm, saying, "Yes, and here to stay." Then he turned toward his brother. "George, my dearest brother, I missed you very much."

"I best be dear to you for all the work I have been doing on your behalf," George chuckled before hugging his brother. "How goes the arm?"

"Not as painful as it was," he replied. "And the wound is not festering, thankfully."

Samuel's mother was eager to dote on him as she led him inside. "Is there anything I can get you?" she asked.

"Perhaps some cider," he replied as he sat at the

table. She nodded and went to retrieve it. "So tell me, how have you all been since you last wrote to me?"

"Good, the crops produced more than we expected this year," his father answered, taking a seat as well.

"I am happy my absence did not disrupt the planting then," Samuel added.

"No, I think the crops liked not having you working them to death this time around," George playfully took a jab at him.

"Well, if I am working hard, so should they," he swiped back. "In all seriousness though, I am glad to see you are all safe. I heard the jails have become crowded with witch suspects."

"Yes, there have been more hangings as well," his father added grimly.

His mother returned with a cup of cider for him. "Thank you," he said as he took a long sip. "Oh, and what became of Goody Parker? The last you told me was that she had been arrested."

His mother and father looked at each other, trying to decide who should give him the bad news. "Will you tell him?" his mother asked her husband.

"Tell me what?" Samuel felt anxious about the way they were staring at each other and not answering him.

His father sighed deeply before answering, "Goody Parker was tried over two weeks ago... and found guilty."

"But that woman is not a witch. Does she still sit in prison?" Apprehension rose within him as he looked upon the sullen expressions of his parents.

"No, Samuel." His mother shook her head sadly. "She was... she was executed."

A pallor formed on Samuel's face and he sank back into his chair. He shook his head, not quite believing what he had heard. "No, please, tell me you jest?" he asked.

"I wish I was, son," Mrs. Galler answered solemnly. "But there is more."

"Oh God, what more?" he sighed.

"Sarah… she too was accused, just this week," she spoke slowly as she watched her son's eyes grow wide. "She is now in Salem jail."

Samuel felt as if the breath had been pushed out of his lungs and he gulped. The joy he had felt previously now crumbled away like ashes in the wind. His beloved was arrested and her mother killed. He had been looking forward to seeing Sarah upon his homecoming and imagined her cheerful face when she laid eyes upon him. Now he suspected he would not be seeing her smile for a long time.

"Dear God, that poor woman," he muttered. "I should go see her. I can do that, can I not?"

"Sam, she may not want you to see her like that," his mother explained. "You may embarrass the poor girl."

"But I do not want her to think I have cast her aside," he retorted.

"Then write to her, and give the letter to one of her brothers at Sabbath meeting," she told him.

"If they even go," his father chimed in. "They did not come to the last after their mother was executed."

"It is understandable why they do not come," his wife said. "It must be torture for them to sit there with the same people who caused their mother's death."

Samuel had ceased listening to their conversation

and was trying hard to come to terms with the news he had received. "Excuse me," he murmured as he got up from the table.

He made his way upstairs to his room as if in a dream, seeming to move outside of his body. For a long time, he sat upon his bed with his head in his hands lost deep in thought. Finally, he thought of just what he wanted to say to Sarah and composed the most heartfelt letter he could muster.

ⳁ

Sarah and Martha stood in a corner of the common room observing the conversations and the visitors received by the inhabitants of Salem jail. Martha was able to relate some of the information she had on the other prisoners. Many, like Sarah herself, were imprisoned for witchcraft and some of them had been here for months. They were in the middle of talking when Sarah stopped suddenly, seeing John and Joseph walk into the room.

"Sarah, glad to see you not confined to a cell for a time," Joseph stated with a smile as he hugged his sister.

"Yes, Martha here insisted we move about some," she returned. When she released him from the hug, she gestured toward Martha. "She is my fellow prisoner. Martha, these are my brothers John and Joseph."

"Nice to meet you, gentlemen," Martha greeted in a flirtatious voice. "You did not tell me you had such handsome brothers."

"Careful there. Are you not in enough trouble as it is?" Sarah replied humorously.

"Well, I cannot help it if there are good-looking men to tempt me," she smirked and eyed up the two men.

"I will have you know I am a married man," John said sternly, finding no humor in her advances.

"I am *not* married," Joseph was quick to interject as he grinned at Martha, who gave him a sideways smile.

"Joseph, please," John sighed before returning his attention to his sister. "Sarah, how have you been faring?"

"I suppose as well as one can living in these appalling conditions," she muttered.

"Is there anything I can bring for you?" he asked.

"Perhaps a blanket? The straw matting is very uncomfortable to sleep on," she replied and stretched her back as if to emphasize the point. Her back was indeed in pain from having to sleep on hard, scratchy straw.

"I will bring one next time," he said. "But for once, I do have good news for you."

"Oh? What is it?" Sarah's tone was skeptical after having received only bad news thus far.

"Samuel has returned from Maine," he announced, pulling the letter from his coat. "He wrote this for you."

Sarah's eyes grew wide as she took the letter from her brother's hand. "He has? Is he unharmed?" she asked, not quite believing it.

"A bullet tore through his left arm, but he said it seems to be healing well, though it pains him every so often," Joseph answered.

"Aw, poor man," she said sadly. She studied the letter in her hands and her next question came out in a weak voice. "Does… he know everything?"

"Yes, and he seemed most despondent about it," John replied. "He was deeply concerned about you. I believe he even wanted to come see you."

"No!" Sarah was surprised at her own abrupt reply. "I just… I do not want him to see me in this condition."

"I understand, but should I give him a message from you at least? I think it would be best for him to hear something from you." John thought back to the younger man's sorrowful, desperate face. "I can give him a letter from you in return."

"I should like to review his letter first," she stated. "For now, tell him that I am most pleased to hear of his return and hope he recovers well… and that… I do miss him terribly." She wanted to add that she would see him upon her release, but she dared not speak of something that may never come to pass.

"Very well, and Ann made you some food." He gave her a wrapped cloth filled with freshly baked bread and small ginger cakes, Sarah's favorite.

"She is an angel! Give her my most sincere thanks," Sarah exclaimed gratefully. The food in prison was less than satisfactory and she missed the savory meals she had at home. She took out one of the ginger cakes and handed it to Martha. "Here, you must try this. 'Tis most delicious."

Martha took the piece and ate it, relishing the taste. "These are good. I would like to thank whoever this Ann is."

"She is my wife," John told her.

"No wonder you are so chaste. No man would dare be unfaithful to a wife who cooks like this," Martha spoke unabashedly.

"By God, who is this woman?" John turned to his sister, flabbergasted by the woman's bluntness.

"A repeated fornicator," Sarah stated matter-of-factly.

Joseph broke into laughter. "Well, that explains a lot."

"Do not fear me, I will keep my hands to myself, I promise," Martha replied, giving John a sly smile.

"Do you take pride in being a sinner?" John frowned at her.

"Only in that I make no pretenses of being a saint," Martha shot back.

"Well, you must admire the woman's honesty," Joseph smirked, liking how Martha made no qualms about telling the truth.

"You seem to, far too much," John chided his brother.

After a time, John and Joseph had to return home and Sarah wanted desperately to go with them. Seeing as she could not, she instead carefully broke open the seal to Samuel's letter.

"So who is Samuel?" Martha asked as she watched Sarah's attention become consumed by the letter.

"He is a man I had hoped to marry," she muttered her response as she began to read the letter. Her eyes scanned slowly over the page as she took in every word. Tears welled up in her eyes as she finished reading the piece of correspondence.

"What is wrong? Does he write of bad news?" Martha asked, seeing the other woman's sudden change in demeanor.

Sarah shook her head. "No, he wrote a beautiful letter…but… he will not want me now." She started to sob uncontrollably.

"Does he mean to cast you aside?" she questioned worriedly.

"He makes no intention of that," Sarah sniffled.

"Then why would you believe he would no longer want you?" Martha was confused by her reaction to his letter.

"Because he will realize that he does not want a woman tainted by a witchcraft accusation." Her words came out in a hurried mess. "Why would he want a woman whose life has been torn asunder? He will see that I am a burden and he will want someone whose life is steady and clean."

"Sarah, I fear you are not making any sense." Martha raised an eyebrow at her. "Would you read the letter to me, please?"

Sarah hesitated for a moment, wondering if the letter was too personal to share. She looked up into Martha's pleading eyes and saw the other woman only meant to help. She took a deep breath to try to control her voice and began to read:

Dear Sarah,

I write to you with the heaviest of hearts after having learned of your most recent misfortunes. When I returned home, I had every hope of seeing you and I longed to see your smile more than anything. You can imagine my despair when I heard of the tragedy that befell you and your family. Your mother was one of the most gracious and kindhearted women I have ever known and I am terribly sorry that her life was taken so unjustly.

I have also been informed of your own arrest. I cannot bear to think of you in prison, for your soul is like mine, it is sustained by freedom. And when you come to know freedom again, I should like to rejoice with you on that day. Until then, do not lose heart, for the sun shines on even the roughest of roads. Please know that not a day will go by when I do not think of you and I will keep you in my prayers always.

Your most faithful heart,
Samuel

When Sarah had finished reading, Martha said, "The man seems to be undoubtedly in love with you and he clearly is pained to know of what happened to you and your mother. I do not know why you think he would suddenly change his mind and want to cast you aside."

"He may think now that he still wants me, but he will realize that he can do better than me," Sarah said as she wiped away her tears.

"Nonsense! Why do you believe the worst when he has given you no reason to?" Martha said. "And he would be a fool to not take a beautiful girl like you for a wife."

"I am not so beautiful now," she murmured sadly.

"Do not be so gloomy. The good Lord knows our circumstances are dire enough without you bringing yourself down further into misery," Martha lightly scolded her.

Sarah folded up the letter and wondered just why she felt so despondent. Samuel made it clear that he was not giving up on her, so why did she think they were no longer destined to be together? She could not explain it other than that a terrible sadness was encasing her soul more and more each day. Every moment she spent in this jail, every time she cut open the emotional wounds from her mother's execution, every hour she spent thinking of the injustice done to her and the others, a new layer of sadness grew within her. She feared that soon it would suffocate her entirely.

CHAPTER TWELVE

Sarah awoke the next morning as sunlight filtered in through the small, barred window of the cell. There was something black in her field of vision near her face and she screamed as the object moved. It was a large rat and it ran away from Sarah just as she jumped up from the floor. She cried out as her leg cramped from the sudden movement. Falling back to the floor, she rubbed the pained appendage.

"What is all that screaming about?" the older woman in the cell, whose name she had learned was Dorcas Hoar, asked in annoyance.

"There was a giant rat," she replied through gritted teeth as she massaged her leg.

"They are all over this prison, nothing to be screaming about," Hoar reprimanded her as she lay back down and turned away from Sarah.

"Forgive me if I am not used to living in filth," Sarah muttered, angered at the woman's lack of compassion.

She heard a muffled voice next to her as Martha

awoke. "What happened?"

"A rat scared the life out of me," she replied.

"Oh yes, they like to come and go." Martha yawned as she stretched her arms.

"Hurt my damn leg trying to get away from it." She stretched her leg gingerly to relieve the cramped muscle.

"Well, do not go killing yourself over them," Martha said wryly.

Sarah only shook her head and continued rubbing her leg. Soon the guards were coming in to bring the prisoners their morning meal. It was dry and unsavory as usual and Sarah only managed to down half of it before she grew sick of the taste. She got up and walked over to the window and stood on tiptoe to look out. There was not much to see, only the fenced-in yard of the prison and the bleak sky. Gray clouds appeared in the distance and it looked as if it might rain. The dreary day complemented her mood. Walking back over to her usual place in the cell, she felt a familiar tickling feeling on her head.

"Why is my head so itchy?" she asked in frustration as she scratched at her scalp. The itching had started a day or so ago and now it was getting worse. She felt something nubby on her hair and pulled it off with her fingernail. Upon examining it, she realized that it was moving. "Oh no, please tell me that is not what I think it is."

"I fear this jail has lice as well," Martha sighed.

Sarah grimaced in disgust and made quick work of removing her cap. She vigorously brushed at her head, trying to get the lice off. She wanted to gag at feeling the small insects in her hair.

"Do not bother, you will not get them all off like

that," Martha stated. "They will just come back anyway."

"It never ends," she groaned. "This is one more thing I have no need to deal with."

"What can you do about it?" Martha sighed and shrugged her shoulders.

"Run away from here is what I would really like to do," Sarah said tiredly as she rubbed her face with her hands. As if being imprisoned for a crime she was innocent of was not enough, now she had to deal with the jail's resident pests. *What did I ever do to deserve this hell?* she thought wearily. *Maybe mother was right when she said I was too vain about my hair and now this is my punishment.* But no, God could have punished her for that sin without confining her to a cell. This penalty was far too harsh for a transgression as small as that.

ଔ

The weather was starting to get colder as the middle of October approached. While the trees began to turn vibrant colors as autumn rolled on, the gloominess in the Parkers' house only increased with Sarah's absence. The family members also now had to do double their share of work with her and Mary both gone. John and Joseph were in the barn this afternoon feeding the horses with hay and oats. A man they had never seen before walked inside and approached them. John stood up straight before the man and grabbed a hammer off the nearby table and held it defensively in hand.

"Who are you?" he demanded of the stranger.

"I am one of Sheriff Corwin's men," the man explained. "He has ordered me to take an account of

Mary Parker's estate in the name of their Majesties William and Mary."

"And why does he need an account of her estate?" John asked angrily.

"Because after her condemnation, her estate became forfeit to the king," the man replied.

"What the hell are you talking about?" Joseph fumed. "We know of no law that allows for one's estate to be forfeited after they are condemned."

"I am afraid that the law indeed allows for that," the man said calmly.

"Any property of our mother's fell to us after her death!" John yelled. "She has no estate left!"

"Do not fool me," the man shot back. "My men and I are to take what is of value."

"You brought others with you?" John pushed past the man and walked outside. He saw two other men leading some of the cattle that had been grazing in the fields toward a cart they had brought with them. He ran up to them, shouting as he went, "What are you doing? You cannot take our livestock!"

Infuriated by the scene, Joseph turned back to the man and roared, "You have taken our mother from us, you have taken our sister from us, and now you want to take our property! For God's sake, do you people have no sense of decency?"

He pushed the man back against the barn wall, but the officer shoved Joseph away from him and held his ground. "I do not do this for my own pleasure," he said. "But I have my orders to take her estate." The man went to the back of the barn where the corn was kept and started to gather it up.

"Do you mean to starve us out before winter, man?" Joseph stood astounded by the man's audacity to steal their crops right in front of him.

The man ignored Joseph and continued on, "Should you not want these goods to be sold, you are to go to Salem and make an agreement with Sheriff Corwin."

"Sold? How are you going to sell what does not belong to you?" Joseph angrily swatted at the man's arm, causing him to drop some of the corn he had been holding.

"If you interfere with my work, I will have you arrested!" the man cried out.

"You can try, but you will have to kill me to do so!" Joseph grabbed the man and hurled him toward the barn door.

The man stumbled and fell despite trying to maintain his balance by grabbing onto one of the work benches. He scrambled to his feet and ran out the door with a hostile Joseph on his heels. The officer called out to one of his men, but Joseph yanked him back by the collar. The man elbowed Joseph in the stomach, but he quickly recovered. He was about to lunge at the man when a shot rang out. Joseph instinctively ducked at hearing the sound and slowly looked up to see another man pointing a musket at him.

"Back away!" the man holding the gun commanded and Joseph begrudgingly walked away from the officer, not taking his eyes off the musket-wielding man. "No one needs to be harmed here. Let us follow our orders," he said.

Joseph glared at him as John stepped in between the two and made a command of his own. "Take what you need, and then get the hell off of our property!"

The brothers were forced to watch as these strangers took their cattle and crops under the guise of the law. Ann and Peter came out of the house, confused as to what was going on. They both became distressed when they found that their property was being confiscated. As they watched the men load the cart up with corn and hay, the Parkers were left wondering just how much more would be taken from them that year.

ଔ

As October wore on, the temperature in the jail dropped and the prisoners suffered an ever-present chill. Despite the cold, Hannah and her husband decided to pay a visit to Sarah as well as to their sister-in-law and niece who were still in jail. Hannah was horrified by the state her poor sister was in. Sarah was no longer wearing her cap and her hair had become disheveled, with pieces sticking out of the braid she normally wore it in. She had dark circles under her eyes and her clothes were dirty. Even though she had a blanket wrapped around her shoulders to keep her warm, she was still shivering.

"My God, Sarah, I cannot bear to see you in this condition," Hannah said as she attempted to put an arm around her sister.

Sarah held her back, however. "Please do not. You do not want to get dirty or catch lice."

"Lice? Is that why you are not wearing your cap?" she asked.

"Yes, between the constant scratching and my hair falling out of it anyway, I no longer see the point of wearing it," Sarah answered. She scratched roughly

170

at her scalp and yelped when her nails dug a bit too deep. Blood coated the edge of her fingernails from having cut herself.

"Careful, do not scratch so hard," Hannah warned.

"I cannot help it. The itching is so irritating," she groaned.

"I am sure, but you will only make it worse by scratching at your scalp." Hannah watched as Sarah wiped the blood off on her skirts.

"Have you heard from our brothers? They have not come for some time." Sarah's voice held a touch of loneliness.

"They have had some difficulties of late," she explained. "Sheriff Corwin sent an officer to confiscate Mother's property."

"What? How can he do that?" Sarah asked, appalled.

"Apparently, the law allows for that once someone has been condemned." Hannah shrugged.

"What did they take? How much of it?" Sarah questioned rapidly.

"According to John, they took quite a lot of the crops and cattle," she continued. "They were told to go to Corwin in Salem. He made them pay six pounds to prevent their goods from being sold."

"Made them pay for their own property!" Sarah shouted. "These people need to burn in hell!"

"Sarah, do not go as low as they and curse others," Hannah chastised her. "God will see to their punishment."

Sarah was tired of people telling her how to feel or behave. "I will speak as I wish," she growled. "I need not wait for God to bring ill on these people when He does naught but bring them satisfaction."

"So you believe God approves of what these people do?" Hannah was taken aback by her sister's brash statement.

"Either He does or He pays no mind to our affairs anymore." Sarah shrugged and turned her face away from Hannah.

Her sister gently touched her cheek and spoke softly. "Your faith has become so shaken, but God will deliver us yet."

"Can God deliver me out of these chains?" Sarah asked with resentment.

"I fear you may not be released for some time," Hannah went on. "Word has come that the governor has halted all court proceedings until further notice."

"Now he decides to stop them? He waited until twenty people died to act." She shook her head. "He waited too long."

"I agree his lack of action led to tragedy, but we can only pray that he does something to stop more people from dying," Hannah said. "And now that he has returned from Maine, John and Joseph have decided to write to him directly concerning their property."

"Let us see if he will actually rectify injustice for once," was Sarah's snarky reply. She had ceased to believe in anything these days.

Hannah grimaced at her sister's pessimistic nature and took her hand. She looked at the red lines that now marked her sister's wrist from the iron chains. Shaking her head, she squeezed Sarah's hand and said, "Sarah, I know what you are going through is difficult, but you shall not perish here. Please believe that your suffering will end eventually."

Sarah laughed darkly and a malicious smile appeared on her face. Cruel humor filled her lowered eyes as she spoke. "Yes, it will end… at the end of a rope."

"Sarah!" Hannah gasped, pulling back from her. "Stop that!"

"It is the truth. You and I know it well." Her words held no hint of mirth now.

"No, do not speak so, please." Hannah shook her head, disheartened by her sister's negativity.

"I am sorry to upset you, but as I am sure you can understand, I have not much to be hopeful for," Sarah spoke soberly.

Hannah only nodded. "I know, but try not to fall too deep into despair," she said. "I am afraid I must go to see my sister-in-law and niece now."

Sarah bade her sister farewell and fought the urge to beg her sister to take her home.

ᑲ

Sleep once again evaded Sarah that night. Silently she sat in the darkness of the cell listening to the sounds of her fellow prisoners. Martha breathed heavily beside her, while another woman snored on the opposite side. Something scurried around in the cell and she heard a light screeching noise, most likely belonging to a rat. She had become a light sleeper in this prison, and all of these noises prevented her from sleeping. She often found herself sleeping during the daytime when many of the people would clear out of the cell for the common room.

She sat with her knees to her chest and her chin rested on her arms as she stared out into the darkness.

She was so terribly homesick and longed for her family. How desperately she wanted to run to her mother's arms like she was a little girl again and be comforted by her embrace. Once again, she felt the familiar wetness forming in her eyes as she thought of how her mother would never be able to hold her again. Suddenly, she felt a light pressure on her left arm. The skin there became cold and goosed fleshed. It was then that she had a flashback to when she thought she had seen her mother's ghost in the house.

"You were warning me, Mother, weren't you?" she whispered into the darkness. "When you appeared to me after your death, you were trying to tell me about this, I just did not understand."

As quickly as the sensation on her arm came, it went away, as if to signal that the message her mother had been trying to give her had finally been received. A glint of light caught her eye and pulled away her attention for a moment. She saw the moon shining in the distance through the cell window. The object which once filled her with comfort now brought her vague repulsion. She walked over to the window and gripped the cold bars. A chill ran through her from the draft coming in through the window and she shivered.

"You mock me now, do you not?" she whispered as she gazed up at the moon. "You are free to travel among the stars and I am stuck in this dungeon." She rested her forehead against the cold window ledge and sobbed, "I want my freedom… I want my freedom."

CHAPTER THIRTEEN

October turned to November and the temperatures only continued to decline in the jail. Peter, Ann, and Elizabeth had each finally paid Sarah a visit, but they were unable to bring her any joy. Seeing them only made her long for home all the more. She wanted desperately to be with her family instead of being in this prison. It was tedious and maddening to just sit there day in and day out with nothing to do. She was running out of things to talk about with Martha or the other women whenever they decided to speak. Sometimes she took to weaving objects like flowers or butterflies out of the straw, having nothing else to do. She was accumulating an entire collection at this point.

One day, Sarah was taking a nap when she was awakened by a male voice in the cell that she did not recognize. She turned slightly to look and saw a middle-aged man sitting near Dorcas Hoar. The two were deeply engaged in conversation and Sarah could just make out what was being said.

"So it appears my stay of execution will be longer than expected," Hoar said.

"Yes, and so more time for you to prepare your soul for eternity," the man replied.

"I feel that I am ready now, but will you pray with me for a time?" she asked.

Sarah turned to Martha. "Who is that man?"

"Reverend John Hale. He comes from Beverly. Goody Hoar is his parishioner," she replied.

Sarah looked back at the two who were now engaged in prayer. The man's conviction and the face of Hoar as she solemnly prayed with him sickened her. She felt embarrassment for them that they could still have faith in something so useless. She just shook her head and turned back on her side to face the cell wall. After what seemed like an eternity, the voices ceased. She turned and sat up on the straw matting and noticed Reverend Hale coming toward her and Martha. As he came closer, she got a better look at him. He looked to be in his fifties with gray strands sprinkled throughout his brown hair. A few wrinkles were etched into his face, but there was a kindness to his eyes that gave him a warm aura.

"Miss Upton, still here I see," he spoke to Martha first. His voice was firm, but there was a hint of sympathy in it.

"I fear my family has still offered me no reprieve," she said.

"Have you been in contact with them at all?" he asked.

She shrugged tiredly. "I have neither heard nor seen from them in weeks."

"Can you write to them or have someone do so for you?" he spoke with concern. "They cannot leave

176

you here forever."

Martha snorted. "You do not know my family then. I doubt if they would even respond to anything I sent them."

"It doth not hurt to try," he advised.

"I will think about it," she replied.

He nodded at her and then turned toward Sarah. "And I have not seen you before. May I ask your name?"

"Sarah Parker," she said tiredly. "Martha tells me you are Reverend Hale."

"I am. Forgive my bluntness, but are you related to either of the Parkers who were executed?" he asked.

"Yes, my mother was Mary Parker," she replied sadly.

"I am sorry for your loss. It was a tragic turn of events," he said. Sarah eyed him with suspicion, but his tone seemed sincere.

"It was, though I suppose I will follow her to the grave soon enough." She cast her eyes down. "Another victim of their pretenses."

"So you deny the accusations against you?" he questioned.

She nodded. "I am thoroughly convinced all such accusations are false."

"The truth will be made visible. It is inevitable," he replied.

"Do you believe them?" she asked pointedly.

Her question caught him off guard and he answered in the best way he could. "I believe there may be trouble plaguing the afflicted, but I am not certain if it is the work of witches or if the devil himself harms the afflicted and brings blame to the innocent."

"I will tell you now, it is neither," she remarked. "There is no need for witches or devils to turn man against man; they are perfectly capable of it on their own."

"Sadly, you are right," he sighed. "But I do not believe the afflicted would knowingly plead falsely against those they accuse. Still, you must continue to pray for resolution."

"I cannot pray to someone who is not listening." Her voice became tense.

"Do you not believe in God?" he asked and narrowed his eyes at her as if he were testing her moral character.

"'Tis not that I do not believe in God, sir, I just doubt that he cares," she answered solemnly.

"You feel God has abandoned you?" It was more of a statement and less of a question.

"He abandoned all of us a long time ago," she returned. "Otherwise twenty innocent people would not have been killed."

"I cannot truly speak to their guilt or innocence, but I believe the court tried their cases to the best of its ability," he explained. "But we must not lose our faith. God hath his reasons for the tests that he imposes on us all and surely at the end of our journey we will see his reasoning."

"What reason could possibly exist for murdering my mother?" she asked, suddenly glaring at him as she stood up." You know, I prayed. I prayed so hard, day and night, after my mother was taken into custody. I prayed that something, *anything*, would save her life, and no salvation came for her. She died anyway, murdered unjustly."

He was silent for a moment as he tried to think of something to tell her. He had faced similar questions by others who had been dealt the worst outcomes of the trials. Yet, there was something about the look in the woman's eyes that had him at a loss for words. It was not the anger in them that bothered him, but something deeper, beyond that. It was as if all hope had been ripped from her body and all that was left was a broken shell. Her eyes seemed to challenge him to prove that such hope could be replaced, and he wasn't entirely sure that it could.

"I did not know your mother and therefore do not know the entirety of her life," he said. "But perhaps now was just her time to depart this world. I know you are ill content with the way she died, but if your mother truly was innocent, then you have no reason to believe that she is not now at rest in God's kingdom."

"But she deserves to be here! If God kills his most devoted followers, then that is no God I mean to follow!" Her harsh words stunned her fellow prisoners as a shocked gasp sounded through the room.

"You must not say such a thing," he said weakly as she had even managed to make the minister's resolve crumble at her words.

"I am tired of people telling me what I must and must not say! How I should and should not feel!" she yelled. "You don't know me. You do not know what I must suffer day in and day out! You do not know the thoughts, these horrible, terrible thoughts that fill my mind. I will do whatever I feel is necessary to get myself through each miserably long day here and I will not be told otherwise."

"Please try to remain calm." He tried to reason with her.

"No! Just leave me alone!" she cried. "Go away!" She fell back down to the floor and turned to face the cell wall. "I just want to be left alone! Please, just leave me alone." Her cries once again turned to sobs. She clutched her knees tightly to her chest as she broke down yet again.

Ë

As more time passed, Sarah settled into a distressing daily routine. She would wake up with the most intense feeling of dread and with her stomach in knots. Then she would try to steel herself for the coming day, but by the afternoon she would be reduced to tears. Her crying would be so intense that she would find herself dry heaving and having trouble breathing. It would end with a severe headache at which point she would try to find sleep to relieve the pain, but sleep did not come easily to her. Then the next day she would feel angry and frustrated and nearly to the point of shaking and screaming out her rage. By the third day, she would feel exhausted and bored, and then the cycle would repeat all over again. It was a tiring existence.

At first, she had tried to hide her tears from the other women, but after awhile she stopped caring. *Let them judge me, let them stare, let them make snide remarks,* she thought. *They are no better than I.* Most of the time, with the exception of Martha, no one said anything and her crying was ignored. She was unsure how to feel about that. Part of her wanted them to leave her be, but part of her wanted some acknowledgment of her pain, some comfort, or even a kind word. The silence could be unbearable. But these women were not her family, they hardly knew her, and they were in the same, if not a worse, situation as her. They owed her nothing and they were under no obligation to comfort hurt.

Yet, the feeling of being alone in her grief was hard to bear. She wanted to scream out just how miserable she was. She felt the pressing urge to open her heart and say every single thing that was hurting her. She wanted desperately to cling to her mother or brothers or sisters, but they were not here. They could not envelop her in their warmth and make her feel better. She could only depend on herself and she had to get herself through this.

The only question on her mind now was when would it end? She had since begun to lose track of just how many weeks it had been. The days and nights became blurred in prison. All she wanted to know now was just when she would be given a trial. They would most certainly find her guilty and hang her. *Death would be better than this hell,* the grim voice in the back of her head whispered. The endless waiting was wearing her down. She hoped for them to either release her or kill her. She couldn't take one more day of this infernal prison, but there was never any news. Her fate hung in the balance and it was not knowing when her ordeal would end that was the hardest part to suffer. Until they decided what to do with her, she was left to waste away in this purgatory.

And waste away she did. When she would finish the food her family brought her, she would have to eat the food provided by the jailer, which was not as plentiful as she had been accustomed to. The small portions the prisoners were given were barely enough to sustain them. With the colder weather, the visits from her family became sparse as well as did the food they brought with them. Even the fluids she was given had to be rationed so as not to drink them all before more was given. More still, there were days when she made herself so sick from crying that she was unable to stomach the food anyway. She found herself growing weaker and thinner. The only saving grace was her limited activity so she did not have much energy to lose.

The shackles were driving her mad as well. The limited movement they allowed was annoying her and the heaviness hurt her arms so badly that she often had to refrain from lifting them. Several times she had tried to pick the locks with whatever was available to her, but they would not open. One day she pulled furiously at the chains, trying in vain to break them off her wrists. She pulled on the middle of the chain with her foot, while her hands pulled in the opposite direction. She screamed in frustration when that too had failed.

"What on earth are you doing?" Martha asked in fear for her companion.

"I want it to be over with!" Sarah cried out. "I want it to end!"

"Hush, Sarah, please." Martha tried to soothe her. "You do not want to work yourself up again."

But Sarah only continued to wail, "I cannot stand it anymore!"

"I have been here longer than you and far longer than I need have," Martha said. "Do you think I do not want it to end? None of us can bear this, yet we must. We cannot let this place break us."

"Then it is too late for me," Sarah sobbed. "They have gotten what they wanted. They have destroyed me."

"No, they have not," Martha stated firmly. "You are stronger than that. Do not let them win."

"But I do not feel strong." She shook her head sadly knowing that she spoke the truth. She felt as if she had no fight left within her. She was exhausted, with all of her strength spent on mourning her mother and now her own life.

She resolved right there and then that if the court would not decide her fate, she would decide it for herself. She looked at the shackle on her wrist. It had already dug into her flesh, leaving it raw and bloody. If she pressed down, just hard enough, the shackle would cut through her remaining flesh and through her veins. The blood would pour out. It would be a slow death, perhaps painful to a point, but it would be over. She would be released from this hell.

She waited until night fell and darkness had overtaken the cell. In the dark, no one would see her bleeding out and no one would try to save her. They would find her cold, stiff body in the morning. She waited until she could hear no more movement within the cell, indicating that everyone else was asleep. Carefully, she pressed down on the metal band around her wrist. *You are committing a most grievous sin that you will burn in hell for*, a voice in her head warned her. She immediately answered, *I am already in hell.*

A hiss escaped her lips as the metal dug into her already raw skin. She started to shake both from the pain and anxiety and soon her hand dropped. She sighed in frustration and rested her head against the wall. She couldn't do it; she couldn't take her own life.

Her courage had failed her and the inextinguishable human desire to live prevailed. Then the image of her siblings came to mind. They had already lost so much this year; did they really need to lose her too?

More tears fell from her tired eyes. Her wrist stung from the now exacerbated wound. Fresh blood appeared at the cracked skin. It was enough to cause her additional pain, but not kill her. She dabbed at the wound with her petticoat and pushed the shackle further up on her arm and away from the wound. Once again, she cried herself to sleep.

CHAPTER FOURTEEN

Sarah sat in her bedroom mending a torn skirt when the commotion started. She heard a racket coming from downstairs. She couldn't figure out how to open her bedroom door and had to pull at it for what seemed like several minutes before it finally budged. Cautiously making her way down long, winding stairs, she saw a group of girls shouting and convulsing around the fireplace. They all instantly turned around as she entered the room.

"She chokes me!" the Phelps girl gasped as she clawed at her own throat.

"She pinches me!" one of the afflicted teenagers cried out. The teen pointed her finger and Sarah turned to see her startled mother standing behind her. As if possessed, Sarah rushed at the younger woman like a wild beast. Pushing the teen to the floor, Sarah hurled punch after punch. Bones cracked and screams abounded and soon Sarah could see blood coating her hands.

Sarah awoke feeling sick to her stomach as the memory of the dream coupled with what she had tried to do the night before. She groaned, "Am I still alive?"

"As alive as the day is long." Martha's groggy voice came from beside her.

"Damnit!" Sarah growled.

"Well, good morning to you too," Martha said sarcastically.

Sarah could already feel the sadness welling up inside of her. "Nothing good about it," she sighed.

"Care to share?" Martha had grown used to when Sarah needed to get something off her chest.

"I had a most violent dream last night," she spoke distantly.

"What of?" Martha asked, her tone interested, but her eyes only looking tired.

"They were accusing my mother," she stated bitterly. "They were in my house, those little demon children. They kept shouting at my mother, pointing fingers at her... and I... I just went mad with rage. I attacked one of them, beat her bloody."

"'Tis the pent-up anger," Martha said knowingly. "You look like you barely slept either."

Sarah glanced at the red mark on her left wrist. She felt like vomiting as she thought about what she had nearly done; to think she had nearly taken her own life. *So selfish,* she admonished herself, *to have done that to my family.* She looked down at her lap ashamed and full of grief. Still not willing to admit her careless act to Martha, she thought of a quick lie. "No, I did not; far too many nightmares."

"I have had plenty of those dreams too," she remarked.

"About who? The man who told on you?" Sarah asked.

"No, not about him." She turned away from Sarah then.

"About who then?" Sarah knew she shouldn't pry, but she was curious.

"The people who made me the way I am," she stated matter-of-factly.

Sarah was confused and asked, "What do you mean by 'the way you are'?"

"My incessant need to give men my body. How I continuously ruin my life over and over again," Martha replied sadly.

"Why do you do it to yourself?" Sarah asked her gently. "I mean is it really so important to you that you would put yourself in here for it?'"

"I do not necessarily do it because I like it. I do it because I like the attention and it makes me feel wanted, loved even," Martha explained. "For so long I have felt unworthy of love, and I think if I give myself over to lust, it will bring me love, but I just feel emptier and emptier every time."

"Why do you feel unworthy of love?" Sarah was surprised that Martha was being this open about herself and wanted to know more.

"I suppose it started with my parents. My mother was rather neglectful and my father was perhaps far too… affectionate, in all the wrong ways…" Her voice trailed off at the end.

The implication in her statement made Sarah's eyes widen in horror. Suddenly she forgot about her own troubles for the time being and put her full focus on Martha. She dared not ask her the specifics though, for she had no desire to know and Martha would not want to share anyway. "Did you ever tell anyone?" she questioned.

"How could I? I could have brought my family to ruin," she stated. "And besides, I always feared no one would believe me, or worse, that the blame would have been laid at my feet."

"How long did this go on for?"

"It started when I was ten or eleven, and it continued until I was seventeen," she replied. "That is when the bastard finally died."

"Dear God," Sarah murmured. "And in all those years, no one in your family noticed what was happening?"

"If they did, they never said anything," she answered. "I always had the feeling my mother knew, and I hate her, Sarah. I hate her for not protecting me." A solitary tear trickled down Martha's face as her eyes became watery. It was the first time Sarah had ever seen her break down. "But I think I hate myself more than anything. Even if deep down I knew that what he was doing to me was inappropriate, I thought he was showing that he loved me by giving me so much attention. It was not until I was older that I realized what he was doing was wrong, that it was not really love. But by then, I had already let him ruin me. I feel so soiled, so dirty. Now, I only think I am good enough if I let people use my body and I keep telling myself it will bring me love, but it never does… it never does."

"But you deserve to be loved," Sarah told her. "And you did not deserve what happened to you. You are a good person. You have done so much for me in these past few months just to keep me sane. Even my first day here when you knew me not at all, you still helped me in my moment of weakness. I wish you would not think so poorly of yourself." She had always assumed anyone guilty of fornication must be easily given to temptation. Hannah had admitted to as much when she found herself too impatient to wait for marriage. Sarah never would have imagined that someone's promiscuity could stem from past trauma.

"I wish I had family members who appreciated me as much as you do," Martha lamented and Sarah's heart broke at her words.

"Then maybe it is time you told your siblings the truth," Sarah said. "If you did, then perhaps they can see that it is care you need, not punishment."

Martha shook her head at this. "No, I could not. They would not believe our father capable of that. They would say I was making up excuses for my behavior."

"You need to make them understand what you went through," Sarah explained. "They need to see why they cannot leave you here."

"How can I do that when they do not even come to see me?" Martha was beside herself.

"You must write to them and make clear the urgency of needing to see them in person," Sarah continued to encourage her.

"But… but I cannot write," she murmured.

"I will write the letter for you, and even help you with what to say," Sarah said. Seeing that Martha was still hesitant, she added, "What is the worst that happens? That they neither reply nor believe you? Either way, it does not change anything."

"That may possibly be worse, that is, if I have to keep staying here, but I will try," she finally conceded.

Sarah was glad to hear it. She requested writing materials from the jailer and she sat with Martha and penned a letter for her. Together they made it sound as if there was an urgent matter that required her family to come right away without giving away too much. They also tried to inspire feelings of guilt in what they wrote without sounding accusatory. When they were finished, the letter was sent on its way and then it became a matter of waiting for a response. In the meantime, Sarah reflected on what Martha had told her and wondered just how many people were hurt by the painful secrets they kept.

ের

With great fatigue, John dressed for his journey to Salem. Although, he had to admit, it would be nice to leave the ever-present gloom of the house behind for awhile. Peter was outside readying the horses as they were to go together. Jacob stood nearby and watched forlornly as his father readied to leave. "Can I not come with you?" he asked.

"I am sorry, son, perhaps another time," John replied. He had originally wanted to take Jacob to see his aunt, but after seeing how far Sarah had fallen into despair and the miserable condition she was in, he thought better of it. He didn't think it would be good for his child to see one of his family members like that.

"But what if I do not get another chance to see her?" Jacob pouted.

"What do you mean?" John's face contorted with concern. The little boy's composure failed him and his cheeks became tear-stained. "Jacob?"

"What if they kill her like they killed Grandmother?" he sobbed out.

"Oh, Jacob, no." He bent down to take the boy into his arms. "That will not happen. I promise you."

"You promised me they would not hurt Grandmother and they did," he reminded John.

The older man sighed. "I know and I am sorry. The truth is, I cannot tell you what will happen, but I can promise you that I will fight to keep Aunt Sarah from harm." Jacob only nodded and kept looking at his feet. "Would it mean a lot to you if you went to see your aunt?" John asked. Jacob nodded his head vigorously and John realized he could at least do this for his son if he was unable to give him any other assurances. "Very well, go get your cloak, make haste."

Jacob smiled up at his father and then ran to get his cloak. John hoped his sister would be able to hold it together for the time they were there. When they arrived at the jail, Sarah was brought out to them in the common room. She looked worse each time they came, but John was glad to see her smile when she spotted her nephew.

"Aunt Sarah!" Jacob ran up to her and threw his arms around her legs.

"Jacob," Sarah said just as happily. She returned his hug, before remembering how dirty she was. She pulled away without trying to make it seem like she was pushing him away. "How I have missed you!"

"I have missed you too, very much!" He gave her a wide grin. The child's excitement was infectious, but Sarah dared not let herself feel joyful in fear that it would make her hopeful for good news. "We all miss you at home."

"I would certainly love to be home with all of you." She tried hard not to let her emotions show in front of the little boy. "How have you all been faring?" she asked, turning to her brothers.

"Well enough," John said. "And you?"

"No better than before," she muttered.

"Do you need anything?" he asked.

"A key." She let her sarcasm out as she lifted her shackled hands.

"I wish, this way I would not have to do your chores anymore," Peter chimed in. "Although, I must admit I am accumulating some impressive sewing skills in your absence."

"You with a needle and thread? Lord help us. We will be wearing sleeves on our legs," she laughed.

For a moment, Peter felt like he had been transported back to Andover and they were all sitting around the fireplace talking. He felt a sad nostalgia that came out in his voice. "I have missed your humor."

Sarah saw the melancholy in his eyes and felt pained by how much her family had been impacted by her imprisonment. And so instead of talking about how despondent she felt, she turned the conversation to more ordinary topics. They talked about the latest gossip, local politics, and even the weather. She didn't care what it was, as long as it made her feel normal again for a time.

❧

A few days later, the jailer came in to fetch Martha. At last, two of her siblings came to see her in prison. Sarah gave her some final words of encouragement before she left for the common room. Sarah quietly hoped for the best from Martha's meeting with her family members. In her friend's absence, Sarah went to look out the window. There was not much to be seen, just gray skies overhead and some bare trees in the distance. A solitary bird flitted by and Sarah felt envy for the small creature; how she wished to spread her own wings and fly away.

Behind her, the cell door opened again and she recognized Goody Hoar's voice as the older woman returned to the room. Turning around, Sarah could see that she was once again conversing with Reverend Hale. Tremendous guilt rose up inside of Sarah as she looked at the man. She had reacted so violently toward him the last time he was here and she felt horrible. He was turning to leave when she began to chase after him, her feet moving faster than her thoughts.

"Wait, Mr. Hale!" she called out. "Please, I must speak with you!"

The man stopped in his tracks and seemed perturbed upon seeing her. "Miss Parker," he said firmly, his lips a thin line.

"I… I wanted to… apologize… for my behavior towards you… when last you were here," she stuttered before finding her voice. "I let my anger get the better of me and I unfairly lashed out at you. Please forgive me; I have not been myself of late."

His expression softened upon hearing her words. "I forgive you. Your anger is understandable given your circumstances."

Sarah nodded, but she wanted to say more. With Martha having unburdened herself so recently, she felt like doing the same. Hale seemed to sense this and asked, "Anything else on your mind?"

Sarah sighed. "Oh, there is a lot," she said. "Though I fear you would not want to waste your time on me further."

"One of my duties is to help those feeling burdened in their soul. If you wish to tell me what troubles you, I would listen," he said sincerely.

"I do not think I could," she replied quietly.

"Perhaps you should try," he said.

"Forgive me, but I doubt there is anything you could say to help me," was her sad response.

"Give me a chance?" he tried again.

Sarah wondered why he seemed so determined to help her. He didn't even know her and after her conduct last time, she would have thought he wouldn't want to be anywhere near her. But if he was so determined, she figured she could at least speak with him. She nodded to his question and the two sat together on a bench in the common room.

"I would assume there are a number of things on your mind, but what troubles you the most?" he began.

She sighed. "Being in here. I hate it so, so much."

"Understandably; I hate stepping foot in this place as much as you hate being in it," he said. "The filth alone would drive you mad."

She nodded. "But that is not even what bothers me the most; it is that I cannot leave. I have to stay here day in and day out, doing absolutely nothing but wasting away in body and mind. I crave to walk among the fields again, to see the sunshine, or feel the wind on my face."

"You want your freedom," he stated.

"More than anything… well, almost anything…" she murmured.

"What else would you want?" he asked.

"My mother to still be alive." She cast her eyes down. "Is it strange for one to not accept their loved one's passing? I know it happened, but I still find it so hard to believe."

"Not at all. Loss is difficult for us to come to terms with. It can take much time and self-reflection before we can truly accept it and go on with our lives," he explained. "I imagine it is harder for you. You have not been able to properly grieve for her, being forced into an uncomfortable setting and surrounded by strangers instead of being in your own home with your family able to give you support."

She nodded. "I miss my family and I miss being home so much. I do not know how to get through this without them."

"Unfortunately, you will have to depend on yourself in this situation." He took a moment to breathe before he continued, "When I lost my first wife and eldest daughter, I remember how devastated I felt. And being in my position in the community, despite how horribly I felt inside, I still had to lead my congregation, had to put a mask on and act like I was strong even though inside I felt anything but. So I had to find a way to pull myself out of that darkness. I reminded myself that death was not the end. Perhaps the end of the physical body here on earth, but that the spirit lives on. And my wife and child being the good and pious people that they were, I know that God would have chosen them to be in heaven and I take comfort in that."

"My mother was a good, devout person too," Sarah said after listening to his story. "She lived quietly, never got into any kind of trouble or conflict, so I suppose that is why I find it hard to fathom how she was among those accused, that she of all people was executed. And she was innocent. I know you may not believe it, but she was. She would never hurt anybody, and she most certainly would not renounce God to do the devil's bidding."

"I do not doubt it. She did not confess, did she?" he inquired.

"No, she did not."

"Then perhaps God was testing her conviction in the face of adversity. And if you know your mother to have been truly innocent, then she would have passed that test, and maybe you too can take comfort in the possibility of her being in heaven now," he reasoned with her.

Sarah was surprised at how much his words mirrored her mother's own when Mary had explained why she refused to confess. "I am curious as to why you so readily agree with the possibility of my mother being innocent," she wondered aloud.

He cast his eyes down and responded, "Truth be told, I have found myself questioning the validity of these accusations for some time now. Some of the things I have seen and heard have made me lose faith in the way the proceedings have worked. Even some of those who are accused seem unlikely to be working in witchcraft, least of all my current wife."

"Your wife was accused?" Sarah asked as he nodded. "Was she imprisoned?"

"No, thank the Lord," he answered gratefully. "I, apparently, was not the only one who found the accusation outlandish."

"It seems they have finally made a step too far," she commented.

He looked down at his hands. "Indeed, but I still fear for her safety."

"As you should; never think yourself safe. I was foolish to think I would be safe after my mother died." Sarah shook her head, remembering the day they came to arrest her. "But I guess I was never really safe, not even in my own mind. When my mother first died, I kept having dreams where I was saving her or she would be sick and I would nurse her back to health. Then she was all right, she lived, and we were all happy again." She sniffled to stop the tears from flowing. "Then I would wake up and feel sad all over again… and then the anger would appear."

"Yes, you already showed me some of that," he quipped.

"I know, but I find it so hard to control." She shook her head. "It just consumes me. I even dream about hurting them, the ones who hurt my mother, the ones who hurt me. I want them to feel the pain that I feel, I want them to feel the pain that they put my family through and so many others." Her voice started to rise in frustration. "I want them to know the despair that comes from having your loved one murdered! I want them to know the indignity of being chained in the dark like an animal!"

Her eyes were ablaze and Hale found it terrifying. The dark circles under her eyes and her gaunt face heightened the haunting glare. She appeared as one who had gone mad and perhaps she finally had. She hadn't realized she had been clutching her chained hand so tightly and when she finally released it, deep impressions had been made by her nails, nearly to the point of breaking the skin.

At first, Hale was unsure of how to soothe her anger, fearing he might say something that would make her lash out at him again. Then he asked cautiously, "Do you think revenge would make it all better?"

She nodded and said in an eerily calm voice, "I have nothing else left."

"But once you have taken your revenge, what then will you be left with?"

"Peace." She did not hesitate in her reply.

"Are you so sure?" he continued to question. "You may find yourself feeling rather unfulfilled, perhaps even regretful. How would hurting them make you any better than they?"

"Because it would be justice!" she exclaimed. "I seek justice for the murders they have committed."

He was about to say something about how justice for the executed should be left to God, but he stopped, remembering the last time God came into their conversation when she was angry. Instead, he said, "There is a fine line between justice and revenge, take it from one who knows."

She cocked her head to one side in curiosity. "What do you mean?"

"Goody Hoar. I do not come to visit her just because she is my parishioner, but because I feel partly responsible for her impending death." He met her gaze with sad eyes.

"How so?" Sarah asked in confusion.

He forced himself to continue. "Several years ago she had admitted to me to dabbling in fortune-telling after people began whispering about her doing so. But that was not all; I found out that one of my servants and Goody Hoar's children were stealing from my house. Hoar was the recipient of some of these stolen goods. My daughter knew about this but she was threatened with violence and told that Hoar was a witch, so she said nothing at first. I told the court this information and this woman has now been condemned to death."

"And now you regret saying anything?"

"Yes. I and a few others petitioned the court to stay her execution. It appears, thankfully, that they have stayed it longer than we had requested," he finished.

So he is compensating for his guilt, she thought. "Well, you managed to save her life, at least for a little while. And to be fair, I would be angry too if someone threatened my child," she said sympathetically. There was silence between them for a long time before she spoke again. "Why do we do these things to each other?" she asked. "Why do we harm each other? Would it be so hard for us to care for one another as we do ourselves?"

He sighed. "I wish I had an answer for you, but it seems we have fallen short of walking the path of virtue."

"And now God is punishing us for it," Sarah finished.

"Or perhaps He is showing us that we are wrong in how we go about trying to root out the devil so that something like this will never happen again. Sometimes, only tragedy can lead to change," he explained.

"Loathsome to be on the wrong end of it though," Sarah muttered. "What was done to me, to my family… the community that we put so much faith in ruined our lives. They tore us apart and they will not even bother to mend the damage they created."

"This experience doth not have to be the end of your life Sarah, do not let it be. You are still so young with so much more to experience," he advised.

"You are assuming that I will make it out of this alive," she replied dryly.

"For some reason, I think you will." He gave her a small smile.

"Even if I do not, death would be a relief," she sighed as she sank down where she sat.

"Do not be so quick to take comfort in eternal sleep. If you look hard enough, there is a lot that life can offer you. You can find beauty even in the smallest of places," he mused.

"I suppose I will just have to go out looking for it when I am free one day," she said, trying to sound more cheerful.

"Yes, do so with great enthusiasm." He got up then. "I will not be coming more. My wife is due to give birth soon and I intend to be at her side."

"Of course, I wish her and the baby a safe delivery." She gave him a sincere smile.

"Thank you, and take care," he said.

"And thank you for listening. Farewell." He nodded and turned away. Sarah watched him leave and leaned back against the wall, contemplating their conversation.

Sarah reluctantly returned to the cell, feeling somewhat comforted by the minister's words. Martha finally returned to the cell as well and looked much more optimistic than when she had left.

"Well, how did it go?" Sarah questioned.

"As I feared, at first they did not want to believe a word I had to say. But I did as you said and I told them the truth, made them understand how troubled I have been," she explained. "I think they are still skeptical, but they have agreed I cannot stay here."

"So they will get you out?" Sarah suddenly felt excited.

"Not right away, unfortunately." The other woman's face dimmed. "They do not have the funds to pay for my accumulating jail fees, so they will have to find a way to do so and will probably have to seek help from neighbors."

"The fees are ridiculous, it is not as if any of us want to be here," Sarah huffed.

"For all the misery we are in, we should be charging them for pain and suffering!" And finally, both women were able to genuinely laugh.

CHAPTER FIFTEEN

As the weather turned colder, the temperature was nearly freezing in the jail. Sarah never knew that one could have a headache from shivering so much. John brought her another blanket and she and Martha would huddle together beneath it to keep warm. Near the end of December, illness swept through the prison and Sarah contracted it. It started with a scratchy throat which was unbearable with the little drink the prisoners were given. Then it traveled to her nose and gave her a near-fatal fever. It made her sick to the point that for four days straight she found herself in almost constant sleep, too tired and in pain to move except to relieve herself and eat, which Martha demanded she do to keep her strength up. It was during one of these deep sleeps that she had a blissful dream for the first time in months:

The sun was blazing in the sky as the warm summer day wore on. Quietly she stood on the banks of a river, watching as the water gently rolled on by. The small waves glinted in the sunlight. Sarah decided to wade into the stream. The cool water was soothing on her burning skin. Gently she floated as the current carried her downstream. Then there was a cold, wet sensation on her exposed forehead. Confused, she scrunched up her face and tried to shake it off.

She awoke and opened her eyes, still blurry as they tried to adjust to the light. Her head was groggy from sleep and infection and it took her a moment to realize what was going on. Her sister's face finally became clear before her. "Bessie," she whispered in a dry voice.

Elizabeth smiled softly at her. "You have not called me that since you were a child," she spoke softly as she patted Sarah's forehead with a wet cloth.

"Are you really here?" Sarah asked quietly. Such was her state of mind that she feared her sister was only an illusion conjured by sickness.

"Yes, dear, I am," she replied.

Sarah felt tears well up in her eyes. It was a long journey to make from Andover to Salem in the bitter winter, but it seemed her sister was determined to keep her alive. "You do this for me?" Her voice became hoarse with her unshed tears.

"I will be damned if I lose another member of my family to this injustice," Elizabeth stated, her lips set tight.

Sarah gripped her arm, eyes shining with gratitude. "Thank you… thank you," she whispered as a tear slid from her eyes. It caused her to cough something awful though and it hurt her chest. Elizabeth patted her on the back.

"Martha tells me you have been sick for several days now," Elizabeth stated, and Sarah confirmed it with a nod. "What was the last time our brothers visited you?"

"I have not seen them in close to two weeks now," Sarah replied bitterly.

"They should be ashamed of themselves considering the state you are in," her sister snapped. "I will be sure to talk to them immediately."

Sarah wasn't sure what talking to their brothers would accomplish. It was not as if they could cure her illness. She also could not help but feel as if they had abandoned her with how long they had been absent and it hurt. Elizabeth stayed with her a while longer, until her husband, Henry, was urging her to leave. Elizabeth hurried out of the jail determined to see her brothers as quickly as possible.

"Now you want me to take you to your brothers?" Henry asked in annoyance.

"Henry, I have done everything you have ever commanded of me since we have been wed." She turned to him sternly. "But this is one time you will listen to me. My sister is gravely ill and I refuse to let her die. I have already lost my mother, I will not lose her too." She promptly turned on her heel and continued on her way, not bothering to see if her husband was following her.

When she arrived in Andover, she met similar resistance from her brothers. "When is the last time you have gone to see our sister?" she asked them.

"Perhaps two weeks ago or so," John replied as he tiredly rubbed his cheek.

"And you have not seen her since?"

"We have been busy here. Let me remind you that we are short two sets of hands," he replied. "And the weather has not made travel easy."

"Well, while you worry about the household and the roads, I worry about our sister's health." Elizabeth cocked an eyebrow at him. "Sarah is ill. She could hardly move or speak when I saw her. I fear she will not survive if she is forced to stay in jail any longer."

"And what would you have me do?" he asked wearily.

"Have her released!" She raised her voice at his lack of urgency. "Many families have submitted notes of recognizance and the court has allowed the imprisoned to be released. You must do the same for Sarah."

"Have we not had enough of these vicious scoundrels running the court harassing us?" he countered. "Now you want me to pledge pounds to them and run the risk of them coming to collect?"

"They will only collect if Sarah does not appear before the court as instructed," Elizabeth said.

"What if she is too ill to come?"

"I am sure allowances can be made," Elizabeth sighed. "And if she fails to appear, I can help pay for whatever amount you post."

"Oh, will you now?" Henry chimed in.

"Use my dowry towards it," she stated firmly before turning back to her brothers.

"If she is as ill as you say, Elizabeth, then we need to get her out, John. We cannot lose her as well. No amount of money is more important than her life," Joseph pleaded to his elder brother.

John nodded solemnly and said, "We will go to Salem tomorrow."

He proved as good as his word when he and Joseph appeared at Salem prison the next day. They showed the keeper their approved request for recognizance and he grumbled about the fees he was owed. With the help of their relatives, the brothers had managed to gather just enough money to pay the rest of Sarah's fees, expecting that the jailer would want payment before he let her go. The man counted the money before taking them to their sister. As they made their way toward Sarah's cell, they hoped that her condition had not worsened. The jailer opened the cell door for them and they became worried when they saw their sister looking grimly pale, asleep on the floor. When Martha shook her awake and she saw her brothers, Sarah assumed Elizabeth must have talked to them. Blinking a few times, she watched as they came to her side.

"John, Joseph," she muttered. She was shocked, however, when the jailer came to her and unlocked the shackles around her wrists. The relief of no longer having the heavy irons weighing her down was a welcome feeling. Through weak eyes, she looked up at her brothers. "What's going on?"

"Elizabeth told us how ill you were," John explained as he helped her to her feet, "The court has allowed you to be released after we submitted a note of recognizance on your behalf."

"Released?" she questioned, not quite believing her ears. "Surely I am dreaming."

"I can assure you this is no dream," Joseph said while he helped support her as she stood on shaky legs. "You are going home."

"Home," she repeated. The word seemed a foreign concept to her now, but she could not wait to be there. Finally, she would be able to rest her head in a clean, safe, comfortable place. Her brothers were about to walk her out of the cell when she stopped suddenly. She turned and threw her arms around Martha.

"Thank you for everything, my friend," she said.

"Well, at least one of us is finally free now." Martha returned her embrace. "You take care of yourself."

"I hope you will follow soon after," Sarah spoke softly. "Remember, this too shall pass."

The women gave each other bittersweet smiles as Sarah turned away. She felt bad about leaving Martha there, but now that she had the chance to leave, she wasn't going to waste it. John placed a cloak around her shoulders and the brothers led her out of the cell. She could only stare ahead at the door to the jail as she walked through the common room, for on the other side of that door awaited her freedom. Upon stepping out of the prison, she was blinded by the sunlight. Her eyes had not seen full daylight in months and she had to shield them. And then it hit her... and the tears flowed. "Free, I am free, finally free," she said in a broken voice. She had never shed such happy tears in her life. All the sorrow, the joy, the relief, the pain, it all came out of her in one torrent of emotion. She stopped walking for a moment and bent down to pick up some of the snow still on the ground. She studied it as if she had never seen it before, ignoring the chill it brought to her uncovered fingers.

"I never thought I could be so happy to see snow again in my life," she sobbed.

"Sarah?" She heard Joseph's concerned voice behind her.

"Forgive me, I should have never taken my freedom for granted." She stood back up and turned back to her brothers. "I never thought that being able to walk among snow would be such a luxury."

"I thought you hated snow. John, are you sure this is our sister?" Joseph questioned playfully.

"I am not so sure myself of who I am anymore," she murmured somberly. Sometimes she felt as though she were living someone else's tormented life. Everything she thought she had known, all of her self-assurance and security in her family and community, had been torn to shreds. Now she had to find a way to return to the person she was supposed to be, but how could she when she would never be that person again?

"Never mind that now," John stated, as he climbed onto his horse. He offered his hand to his sister to help her up. "Let us worry about getting you home first."

And she smiled at those words. She was sleepy the entire way home, but she was determined to not miss a single sight on the road. She had missed far too much in the last few months and she needed to believe that she was back in the real world again and not lost in a dream. Back in Andover, she was uplifted by the sight of her home. It looked so quaint and welcoming with smoke drifting out from the chimney and a warm light glowing from the lattice-paned windows. Once inside, she was greeted by her sister-in-law and nephews.

"Welcome home, Sarah," Ann said, giving her a soft smile. Her nephews repeated the greeting as they stayed close to their mother. Sarah returned the smiles. The youngest boy seemed to have grown bigger from what she had remembered. Toddlers always seemed to grow so fast. Sarah's attention was disrupted by bounding footsteps coming down the stairs. She turned to see Peter coming straight toward her. Before she could react, he wrapped his arms tightly around her.

"Peter, no! You will get dirty," she scolded him.

"I care not," he replied firmly.

With half-hearted reluctance, she returned his embrace. "'Tis good to be home with you too, little brother," she whispered to him.

൦ൠ

The first thing she wanted to do was clean herself. She removed her dirty dress and underclothes, finally glad to be free of them. Staring at the dirty garments, Sarah decided she wanted no reminders of her time in prison and threw them in the fireplace. She took grave satisfaction in watching them burn. It was like burning out that part of her life.

She turned to step into the wash basin and looked down at her body before cleaning it. Gingerly, she touched the outline of her ribs, which were far too visible for her liking now. Sighing at the sad condition of her body, she took the water from the bucket Ann had warmed for her and lathered up the washcloth with soap. She worked thoroughly to clean the dirt and grime from her body. There was one problem, however; she still needed to wash her hair and remove the lice from it. Groaning at how lengthy a process it would be, she decided to wash her hair last. She violently scrubbed at her scalp and rinsed her hair out multiple times. Taking the lice comb, she tried in vain to get it through her hair, but in its wet condition it was a tangled mess. Frustrated, she gave up with trying and decided that if she could not comb the knots out, she would just cut her hair. Frantically looking around, she found there were no scissors in her room, even having left her embroidery scissors elsewhere, and she would have to go downstairs to get them. She refused to put on any clean clothes before removing the lice, but she certainly couldn't walk around the house naked either.

"Damnit," she cursed. Slowly opening her bedroom door and hiding her body behind it, she looked around to see if anyone was around. Luckily, none of her brothers were upstairs and she decided instead to call for her sister-in-law.

"Ann!" she called down. When the woman finally approached she asked, "Could you please bring me the scissors?"

"Do your clothes need to be mended?" she asked. "I could do it for you while you finish bathing."

"I do not need them for that," she mumbled.

"For what then?" Ann raised an eyebrow, confused at her tone.

"Please just get me the scissors," Sarah replied, sharply.

"Sarah," Ann replied back just as sharply, sensing her sister-in-law was hiding something. "I mean not to meddle in your private affairs, but if something is troubling you, it would please me for you to tell me. I wish only to help you."

Seeing the sincerity in Ann's eyes, Sarah let her guard drop. "My hair... it is too tangled to work through, I... intended to cut it."

"Cut your hair? But you have always prided yourself on it," she replied in shock.

"It is of no importance to me anymore," she said solemnly. She had been through far too much to care about her hair in that way. "Besides, it will grow back."

"You cannot cut your hair," Ann stated more softly. "Let me comb the knots out for you."

"But there is the lice as well. I do not want you to have to touch it."

"I am mother to two boys. I pull all sorts of things from their hair. Lice is of no matter to me," she said. "Now go back into your room and let me work with your hair." Ann used the same commanding tone she did with her own children. Sarah felt her will drop and found herself obeying Ann's command.

"All right, but give me a moment." Sarah closed the door and turned back to her room.

Resigning herself to letting her sister-in-law comb through her mess of hair, she wrapped a sheet around herself and let Ann in. Sarah sat by the fireplace while Ann took her time painstakingly combing and brushing out all the knots and tangles from her hair, only having to cut out some of the worst knots. When Sarah's hair was mostly free of the tangles, Ann went through it slowly with the lice comb, working through small sections at a time. When she wanted to repeat the process a second time though, Sarah stopped her.

"I can do the rest," she said. "Please, Ann, you have done enough. Thank you."

Sarah gave her a soft smile, which Ann returned. She relented and gave the comb back to Sarah. The younger woman found that she had a new appreciation for her sister-in-law and her heart grew more tender toward her. In total, Sarah combed her hair three times to make it as free of lice as possible. When she felt clean enough, she dressed in fresh clothes and wrapped her hair up in a small cloth to dry. She never knew she could take such comfort in something as plain as cleanliness.

Ann helped to dress the wounds left by the shackles on Sarah's wrists. Ann was surprised at the deep cut on her left wrist, but Sarah dismissed it as having pulled on the chain too hard one night by accident. When supper came, she hardly said a word.

She had many questions on her mind of what had transpired in her absence, but she was too focused on eating to voice any of them. The meal Ann had prepared tasted like heaven on earth to Sarah. The richness of it was something she had been deprived of for months. Quickly, she consumed the food, ignoring the ache in her sore throat.

"Slow down, Sarah, no one is going to take your plate from you," Joseph teased her.

"You eat the food in Salem prison and then tell me to slow down," she retorted.

"I would rather not, thank you."

Not wishing to think of her captivity, she turned the conversation to something else. "Whatever came of your petition for the stealing of our property?" she asked.

"We have received no reply," John said dismissively. "Incorrigible bastards, the whole lot of them."

She shook her head. "For those whose duty is to justice, they prefer to dispense so little of it. How have things been otherwise?"

"Fine enough," he replied. "And it seems we will be having a new addition to our family soon." He gave his wife a small smile.

"You are with child?" Sarah turned to Ann.

"Yes, it appears so." Ann gave a smile in return.

"Good, I am happy for you," Sarah said warmly. "I think we could all use some new life in this house."

"Sarah." She turned to Peter, who continued, "Samuel has been asking about you every week at mass. I think he should like to see you."

"Perhaps when I am better rested and no longer ill, I will speak to him." She tried to keep her voice neutral, but deep down she felt sick at the thought of having to see Samuel. She feared what he would think of her after her imprisonment.

Following dinner, Sarah sat in front of the fireplace in her room. The heat coming off from the flames felt good against her body and helped rid her of the chill she had acquired in prison. She had been constantly cold and there was nothing at her disposal to warm herself until now. The flames danced before her eyes and watching them had a strangely calming, hypnotic effect on her. Her head was still heavy with illness and her limbs ached. When she felt herself getting drowsy, she reluctantly got up, not wanting to leave the heat behind. Lying down on her bed, she breathed a sigh of relief. Compared to her sleeping conditions in prison, it felt like she was sleeping on a cloud. Soon she began to drift off into slumber and as she lay in that strange state between sleep and wakefulness, she could have sworn she felt fingers running through her hair and her mother's voice saying, "Rest now, my girl."

CHAPTER SIXTEEN

For the next two weeks, Sarah focused on becoming well again. Ann and her brothers helped to take care of her and eventually her illness passed and she recovered well. She did not leave the house at all, not even to attend Sabbath meeting. Her brothers said that Samuel could barely contain his joy when he heard of her return. She still could not bring herself to face him as she lacked the courage to do so.

The atmosphere in Andover had changed dramatically. The tide had turned against the trials. The town's two ministers and several citizens had written to the court on behalf of the accused. Stephen had signed it on behalf of his cousins, who did not want to stir up anymore trouble by signing it themselves, especially as Sarah's case had yet to be decided. That would soon change now that she had received notice of her court date. It was another blow to her confidence and she was filled with anxiety at having to enter a courtroom again. While she was fretting about this, her brothers were trying to calm her down.

"I have heard that almost everyone who is being tried under the new court has been found not guilty, as they are no longer allowing spectral evidence," John said.

"With the ill luck we have had, I would not be so willing to assume that my case will follow suit," she replied. "Especially as I am the daughter of one they have hanged."

"Our mother's case should have no bearing on yours," he stated.

"That is how it should be, but these people are far too corrupt," she sighed. "They will murder me."

"Sarah, stop thinking that way."

"I expect the worst." She felt her words get caught in her throat before she sobbed out, "I do not know how I can face the court again. I am not strong enough."

"You must be." Joseph took her shoulders and looked at her sternly. "You have survived all that you have endured thus far. You will survive this too, you must believe that."

"I will crumble upon entering the building!" she cried.

"No, you will not. We will prepare you accordingly and you will stand firm before them all. Look at me," he implored her, making her eyes meet his. "Show them they have not beaten you. You can do this."

She nodded as she wiped the tears from her eyes. Facing this next test would be easier said than done.

Still, her brothers prepared her for a possible trial as they had for their mother. When the dreaded day arrived in mid-January, Sarah felt nauseous and her palms were sweaty. She found herself staring into the wash basin in the kitchen. Looking at her cloudy reflection, she was trying to gather up all of her courage.

"You can do this. Be strong, be bold, be fearless," she told herself. "Do not let them have this kind of power over you. They do not deserve it."

Joseph came in to get her and together they walked out of the house. On the entire way to Salem, her whole body felt jumpy and the familiar fluttering returned in her chest. Her breathing became shallower as she walked up the steps to the courtroom. As was the custom, she waited outside until she was called in while her family went inside. She forced herself to go over the defenses once more as she waited. Her hands were shaking with how anxious she was and the long wait was not helping.

Finally, she heard her name called. She was led inside by one of the guards and she swallowed hard as she approached the magistrates. Her body felt clammy and she felt faint but forced herself to stand firm. The atmosphere in the courtroom was calmer this time around. There were fewer people and the afflicted girls were no longer screaming and carrying on. She spotted her family members and Joseph gave her a nod of encouragement. *Breathe,* she told herself as she took a deep breath, *be strong.*

William Stoughton once again presided over the proceedings. His face was a hard mask as she approached him and the other magistrates. "Presented before us is Sarah Parker, single woman of Andover," he announced. "You are charged with practicing witchcraft in the town of Andover and using acts of witchcraft on or about the twenty-sixth of September as well as at diverse other times to afflict, torture, and torment one Sarah Phelps, single woman of Andover."

Sarah spotted the Phelps girl sitting at the front of the courtroom. Sarah expected her to cry out against her at any moment, but this time she was silent and unmoving in her seat with her head down. Her heart pounded and her face heated with anxiety as Stoughton continued, "The indictment for afflicting Sarah Phelps has been returned ignoramus. Therefore, the charge against you is cleared by proclamation and you are to be discharged upon payment of your fees."

She finally breathed in relief and a smile broke across her face. It was over, finally over. She turned to face her family giddily as she was allowed to leave the courtroom. Joseph clapped her on the back in celebration when she made her way over to her siblings. John spoke with one of the court officials about paying the remainder of Sarah's court fees while she walked out with the rest of her family. Despite the cold, she looked up toward the sky and let the wind blow against her face. *Freedom is nothing but blue skies above you,* she mused. With an energetic step, she walked away from the courthouse, leaving it in her past where it belonged. But there was still one thing on her mind: Martha. She had not a word of her friend's fate since she had left Salem.

John eventually joined them outside and Sarah turned to him. "John, I... I need to know what happened to Martha, please," she said pleadingly. "I need to know what became of her. I am worried about her."

"You want to go back to the jail?" John looked at her quizzically.

"Yes, but... I cannot go back in there, I just can't." She turned her head downward. "The very thought sickens me. Please ask for me, please."

He thought about it for a moment before agreeing. "All right, but quickly."

Arriving at the jail, Sarah looked at the monument to her months of torment. The building looked even more imposing and dark as it contrasted with the gray January sky behind it. The painful memories of the place crept back into her mind and weakened her constitution. Her vision went blurry for a moment. She rubbed at her forehead and had to turn away.

"Are you ill?" Peter asked.

"No, no, I am fine," she replied.

"I will be but a moment," John said as he entered the prison.

Sarah turned around, instead setting her gaze on the river just visible on the horizon. She hoped that Martha was not still languishing in the prison. After a few minutes, John finally returned. "Well?" Sarah asked upon seeing him.

"It seems your friend was released," he stated. "Turns out her family came to an arrangement with one of their neighbors. He paid for her jail fees, in return for her services."

"Services?" Sarah gaped. "She has been indentured?"

"I am afraid so," he responded.

Sarah sighed. It seemed Martha had been taken out of one prison only to go to another. She could only hope that Martha's neighbor wasn't cruel and provided well for her. After all, it couldn't be any worse than Salem prison, could it? Sarah thanked John for asking after Martha and asked if they would let her go to the river for a few moments. She made her way down the grassy slope and toward the muddy, icy banks of the river. The waves were softly moving downstream, carrying bits of ice and branches with them as they ran out into the harbor. They glinted in the winter sun in a slow-rolling rhythm.

She closed her eyes, letting the crisp air envelop her. She breathed deeply and whispered, "Carry me away, take me far away from here." Though the day should have brought her relief and joy, a storm continued to rage inside of her.

❧

She thought that now that her ordeal was over, she would be fine and go back to the way she was. But she was wrong... so wrong. It was as if the defenses she had placed up inside her mind to keep herself sane while she was in prison suddenly came crashing down. Now the dark thoughts never stopped. *Life is pointless, there is no hope for the future, why even bother living?* These were the thoughts that constantly invaded her mind. What terrified Sarah the most was that these thoughts were not specific to her situation; they were existential and she often found herself wondering why human existence even mattered at all.

And no matter how much she tried to focus on something else, those negative thoughts would still manage to creep back into her consciousness. It even affected her physically. There was always a knot in her stomach and a lump in the back of her throat now. At any moment she could find herself breaking down in tears. It never mattered what she was doing either. One night as she sat down to eat with her family, she suddenly started to cry and had to excuse herself from the table. It was even hard for her to get herself up each day to begin her chores. She had no energy for anything but crying. The sadness would hit her as soon as she opened her eyes in the morning. At first, her family members were sympathetic and took the time to try to soothe her despair. Ann had even attempted to mix together an herbal remedy for her to "purify her body of the bad melancholic humor," but the concoction had not helped her mental state and only served to make her nauseous. After awhile, her brothers and Ann were at a loss for what to do to help her.

Her present state also made it impossible for her to sit through a lengthy Sabbath service. She hadn't been to mass since September and she was expected to return, but she knew that at any moment she could burst into tears and didn't want to make a spectacle of herself in front of the entire town. She therefore stayed home for several Sundays in a row, which of course did not go unnoticed by the other members of the congregation. Her brothers simply told everyone that her sickness had returned and she was confined to bed. Both of the town's ministers had suggested to them that if no medicinal cure could be found for Sarah that she should fast for a day and set hard to prayer. When John reported their suggestion, she scoffed and ignored it; prayer had not helped her before and she did not see how it would help her now. Soon her other family members grew concerned about her absences at mass. Hannah came to see her and Sarah pretended to be sick and bedridden.

The tenseness permeated the air as Hannah sat on the edge of Sarah's bed. Sarah didn't feel like being disturbed and giving company to someone when she felt so melancholic. Hannah tried her best to glean information out of Sarah, but she found her younger sister to be mum.

"Well, you seem to be looking better," she remarked.

"Well, I certainly do not feel better," Sarah murmured in return.

"Perhaps you should send for the physician," Hannah suggested.

"He cannot help me."

Hannah sighed, realizing she was getting nowhere with her sister. She looked around the room she once used to inhabit too. It had been ten years since she had married and moved in with her husband, but it never seemed that long ago. Time went by so fast, and the older she got the more she wished it would slow down. Hannah continued looking around until her eyes were suddenly drawn to a corner of the room and they became wide with horror. Her whole body stiffened as if she had become a statue.

"Hannah?" Sarah asked, confused by her sister's sudden change in demeanor.

"Where did you get that?" Her voice was uneven as she raised a finger to point at something.

Turning, Sarah looked in the direction Hannah was pointing to and saw the bottle she had unearthed when digging their mother's grave. Sarah wasn't sure why she had kept it. All it did was remind her of that horrid day when her mother's life ended. Perhaps it was the mystery behind the object that stopped her from disposing of it. "It was buried by the oak tree. I found it prior to Mother's burial," Sarah answered her sister's question.

Hannah's face turned white as Sarah confirmed her suspicions. "Oh God, no, no… this… this is all my fault," Hannah rambled. She became hysterical and began to cry into her hands.

Having no idea what her sister was getting so upset about, Sarah asked, "Hannah, what do you know of that bottle's origins?"

When the older woman had composed herself, she answered in a shaky voice, "Several years ago, when I was but a girl, I was very sick. So ill was I that no remedy could be found. I had somehow become convinced that I must be bewitched; that someone meant me harm. My thoughts were so driven because I had recently quarreled with some neighbor girls and their mother made a great show of reprimanding me for it. I thought if I could make them stop, if I could use their own methods against them by creating that charm, then I would heal. After I buried the bottle, I did get well again…" She trailed off for a moment as more tears formed at her eyes. She swallowed hard before continuing, "Now it seems my experimenting with charms has led my family to ruin. God has sought to punish me for not trusting him to bring me to health and instead using the workings of those who would align themselves against Him. And now He has destroyed my family for the very thing I had practiced."

Sarah sat for a moment taking in everything Hannah had said as the other woman continued to sob uncontrollably. "Hannah, stop." Eventually she found her voice. "Your actions did not do this to us."

"But what else could explain it?" Hannah turned to her, then looked down and shook her head. "Why was I so reckless in my youth? First this and then when Daniel and I sinned before we were wed. It must be my fault for my family's misfortune."

"We all make mistakes, but think about it. How could your actions explain the accusations against others who are not your family? The accusers had their own reasons for pointing fingers as they did and I believe that they became so corrupted of virtue that they lied," Sarah tried to reason with her distressed sister. "And Hannah, do you really think God so spiteful that he would punish those who had naught to do with the making of that charm, instead of punishing you directly? Also, why wait so long before inflicting this supposed punishment? I fear nothing you have said makes any sense to me."

"But I have never truly atoned for that sin," she stated. "And God came to rule on this transgression when I had thought myself safe and when I was content with life."

Sarah shook her head. She had grown so cynical of theology and even God himself with all that had come to pass in her life that she did not want to think further on this conversation. "No, Hannah, I do not think God did this to punish you. I believe it is just the opposite. I think that God simply no longer cares about any of us."

Hannah blanched at that. "But Sarah, how can you say so?"

"I know not what explanation I can provide aside from that maybe so many of us have come to sin and turned our backs on Him, that he has now turned His back on us," she replied. "Think about it. How many people are punished for fornication or drunkenness or theft? Are we not supposed to lead good Christian lives? How long was God supposed to forgive us if His children could never learn to obey? Perhaps we were all damned from the start."

"You really have given up on all of us, haven't you?" Hannah now gave Sarah a pitiful look. "'Tis no wonder you lack joy."

"I find there is naught to take joy in anymore." She turned away from Hannah as she tried to stop herself from crying.

"Sarah? What is wrong?" Hannah asked, seeing her sister's contorted face.

"Everything is wrong!" Sarah exclaimed. "My life is shattered and I will never be able to put it back together again."

"Sarah, no it is not," Hannah told her. "You just need to get back to a state of normalcy. Get back into a daily routine, go out and speak with people, do something you enjoy. You will feel better then."

"It is not that easy," Sarah grumbled. "I do not take comfort in anything anymore. Everything I do now fills me with hopelessness. Can you not see? Nothing lies ahead for me in the future. I will not get married, I will not have children. I will grow old and die alone and miserable. I will achieve no great purpose for there is no purpose to life."

"I hate hearing you talk like this, Sarah, and frankly I do not understand you." Hannah shook her head. "I know you have suffered, that is undeniable, but you still have your youth, a family that loves you, a roof over your head, a young man who pines for you, all of which is more than others have. There is so much the world still has to offer you and yet you choose to be gloomy about your life and languish in this bed."

"I do not choose to feel this way, Hannah!" Sarah blurted out. She was angry that her sister was talking to her like it was her own fault that she was experiencing this melancholy. "It is just the truth. I wish I could see the future as anything but bleak, but I cannot. But you do not understand, no one does."

"Sarah." Hannah tried to touch her sister's shoulder, but Sarah just shrugged her hand off.

"You would not know how it feels! You only had to pay a meager fine for a crime you actually committed while I had to spend months in jail for something I was innocent of. So do not speak to me about what the world has to offer me when it has given me naught but grief," Sarah raved.

"Sarah! What has gotten into you?" Hannah sat back in disbelief. Sarah had never spoken to her like this. "Do not speak to me like that. I am only trying to help you."

"Well, you are only upsetting me more." Sarah turned away from her then. "I think it is best if you just go."

Hannah watched as Sarah folded in on herself and cried into her pillow. She didn't know what to do. Sarah clearly didn't want her around any longer and she was afraid of upsetting her more. Hannah took one more lingering look at her sister's crumpled form and walked downstairs. She spoke to John about their sister's mental state, and he told her that this had been going on for weeks now. Hannah could tell he was losing his patience with Sarah, but she could think of no remedy for the situation. All she could tell him was to remember what Sarah had been through and to be gentler with her. He didn't seem to take her advice to heart.

❧

And so this was what Sarah's life had become for the remainder of the winter. Her emotions never lightened. Even when she found something humorous, beneath her laughter lay the hopelessness she always felt now. So many nights she found herself thinking of the past and all of the bad things that had happened to her. From her childhood to her imprisonment, memories of things that had made her feel awful in the past and were now making her feel worse in the present. Sometimes she would feel resentment toward the people who had wronged her; other times she resented herself for letting them hurt her.

She also found it difficult to continue to try to open up to anyone. Sometimes she tried with Ann, but she was often preoccupied with her children or the household chores. Like Hannah, Ann also seemed to make light of Sarah's situation, as if it was just a passing phase, which annoyed Sarah to no end. And then she had noticed her brothers, even Joseph, were growing agitated with constantly trying to get her to stop crying or trying to talk her through her sadness in the same way over and over again, so she stopped confiding in them altogether. Overhearing their conversation one night only confirmed her fears that they believed she had truly gone insane:

Sarah had found it hard to sleep that particular night and decided to take a walk through the house, hoping that would quiet her mind and restless body for a bit. When she got halfway down the stairs, she heard the voices of John and Joseph and stopped dead in her tracks when she realized they were talking about her.

"I cannot bear to see her so sad anymore," she heard Joseph's voice say first. "I know she has suffered greatly, but the worst is over now and yet she seems to not realize that."

"She has lost faith in everything," John's voice came next. "She thinks her life will forever be full of hardships." There was a brief pause, then she heard him sigh. "I sometimes think that God was testing her conviction, but instead of seeing how He delivered her from chains, she only believes that He has abandoned her."

"I know how broken in spirit she must be after what she has suffered, but I know not what to do for her anymore." Joseph sounded tired. "I have not an idea of what to say to soothe her. Anything I do say does not seem to matter."

"That is how *melancholicks* are," John stated. "You can talk to them for hours on end about how irrational their thoughts are, but still their thinking will not change."

"Do you think it will pass?" Joseph asked, a tinge of trepidation in his voice.

"I cannot say," John answered. "Some I have heard eventually recover, but the rest stay that way the rest of their lives."

"I pray that for her sake it passes. I do not want her to go completely out of her wits like our aunt."

So that's what they thought of her now? That she was as ungrateful as any heretic and that she had become crazed like Aunt Mary? Tears stung her eyes, but she forced herself to not let them fall until she walked back to her room, shoulders slumped in dejection. Never had she felt so alone before, not even when she was in prison. And it hurt, to feel like her own family didn't care or understand.

It didn't matter anyway. Nothing anyone said or did could ever make her feel better. They didn't understand what she was going through and how she felt inside. She was crying out for help and no hand was being offered. The darkness was engulfing her very soul and in her despair, she became a wanderer among shadows, unable to find the light.

CHAPTER SEVENTEEN

Another Sunday came and Sarah missed another Sabbath meeting. John was becoming irritated with this habit of hers and searched her out after returning from mass. He did not find her downstairs and knew she would still be in bed. He made his way upstairs and did not bother knocking before entering her room. Sure enough, she was still in bed, not even dressed for the day.

He shook his head and asked, "Are you going to stay in bed all day?" She groaned and pushed her face deeper into the pillows. "Reverend Dane asked if you were still too ill to come to Sabbath meeting," he stated. "I wish not to continue to deceive him."

"'Tis no deceit; I am ill of heart," she muttered her reply.

"I will not pay a fine for you failing to come to mass," his tone became angrier. "You must cease this crying of yours and leave the house."

"Do you think it so easy?" She sat up abruptly. "Do you believe I enjoy feeling this way? I hate feeling this constant sadness, this hopelessness, this feeling that I will never experience happiness again." Her voice broke as tears began to fall from her eyes. "But I cannot just stop it. These thoughts, these dark thoughts, they keep invading my mind. I cannot shake them off."

John sighed and sat on the edge of her bed. "I know that you have faced so much in these past few months. I know how difficult it was for you," he said. "But you cannot go on this way. Your life is not yet over. Do you think our mother would want you to act like it was?"

She shook her head and turned away from him as more tears fell. "I know she would not, but I cannot bring myself to find any peace. And you really have no notion of how difficult it was."

"We all lost our mother," he continued. "And I know what kind of horrid place the jail was, but at least you are free of it now. So many others languish in it still."

"Yes, you who were free to come and go from there as you pleased, you truly know how bad it was," she bitterly replied. "And of course I should be grateful that my stay was only three months, not five or ten or more."

"But Sarah, you are not there anymore," he chided her. "Why do you still think about it?"

"Because the memories are still with me!" She was annoyed by how obtuse he was being about this. "I keep thinking about how I had to spend months in filth with my wrists chained together, being stuck in a small cell with strangers. I was going mad and there was no way out."

"So do you insist on driving yourself mad now?" He looked at her incredulously. "Do you wish to become like our aunt?"

She narrowed her eyes at him. "Is that what you think of me? That I have gone completely out of my mind? I may be out of the jail now, but that does not mean I am free of the torment. You want to know how bad it was? You really wish to know?" She roughly pulled up her sleeve, exposing the deep scar on her left wrist. "I tried to kill myself in prison, John. I would rather have died than live in that hell any longer. And you know what the only reason I stopped myself was? It was you! And Joseph and Peter. I couldn't do that to you all, not after everything else that happened. And you were going to leave me there. If Elizabeth had not come when she did, you would have left me there and I would have died." She curled in on herself as she became inconsolable.

"Good Lord, Sarah," John whispered. He was unable to speak further as he stared at the angry symbol of her desperation. Her pain suddenly became real to him. To think that he had nearly lost two family members, one of her own volition, struck him hard. It pained him deeply to see his sister in such grief that she was ready to take her own life. They had often clashed given their differing personalities, but he loved her dearly and would never want to see her do that to herself.

He felt tears prickle at his eyes. "Sarah, I am so sorry we did not come sooner, but we would never have left you there, I swear." He took hold of her wrist. "But do not ever, *ever* attempt this again. We all need you; we love you."

He pulled her close as her sobbing intensified. A solitary tear rolled down his cheek in a rare display of emotion. He affirmed to himself from that point forward that he would be more sensitive to his sister's plight.

Sarah slowly pulled away. "I am sorry, I… I… do not know what is wrong with me," she said. "I know my behavior is taking a toll on all of you."

"Do not apologize. We just do not want to see you in this constant state of melancholy. But Sarah, you need to get out of the house," he pleaded with her. "The more you confine yourself to solitude, the worse you will get."

She nodded, knowing deep down that he was right. He convinced her to come to mass with them next Sunday. When Sunday came, she was filled with anxiety. Sarah felt her palms growing sweaty as she approached the meetinghouse. The familiar racing of her heart and churning in her stomach returned. She was worried about what people would think of her. Would they stare at her or say nasty things behind her back? Would any of them dare to ask her questions about her absence, or worse, her stay in prison? As she entered the building, thankfully only a few people cared to look at her and no one save for her sisters spoke to her. So many people had turned against the trials and so many families had been touched by witchcraft accusations that it would have been hypocritical of them to say anything to Sarah.

Sarah looked at the pew where Samuel and his family sat. They were all there and she prayed that Sam wouldn't turn around, but he did. Her breath caught in her throat as his eyes met hers. He stood and gave her a big smile as he moved toward the end of the pew. Sarah stopped before him but did not return his smile.

"Sarah, 'tis so good to see you," he greeted her. "I have missed you."

"And I you," she spoke truthfully, but her voice was weak.

"Are you all right?" he asked, sensing her unease.

"Yes… it has just been so long since I have been here," she explained quickly. "It seems I will have to get used to being in society again."

"I understand," he stated, but he did not entirely believe her.

"Forgive me, I must take my seat now," she stated before moving away.

"Of course." He nodded and watched her sad form as she went to sit with her sisters.

The absence of her mother stung as Sarah sat in the pew with no one to her left. This was the first time she had been to mass since her mother's death and it hurt knowing that her mother would never again sit beside her. As she looked around the meetinghouse, she caught sight of some of those who had accused her and her mother. A wave of anger and disgust washed over her. They killed her mother and caused her to suffer greatly and yet here they sat acting like nothing had happened. She wondered if even a flicker of guilt ever crossed their minds. It frustrated her to know that no punishment would be levied against them. They could walk away unscathed from the damage they had caused.

Not wanting to dwell on the past any longer or receive the attention of any prying faces, she turned her eyes down, focusing on her shoes. Out of the corner of her eye she saw a figure slide into the pew beside her. She jumped for a moment as her subconscious mind immediately made her think it was her mother's ghost. Turning, she saw a face she had not seen in many months.

"I meant not to frighten you, but I really wanted to come over and ask how you were," Lydia said as she sat on the edge of the pew beside Sarah. She looked at Sarah with searching, worried eyes. "I am glad to see you again, truly."

"Yes, it has been far too long," Sarah replied. She tried her best to look cheerful at finally seeing her friend again, and part of her was as she realized just how long she had been without her company.

"I am so sorry about your mother; it was terrible what they did to her." Lydia looked sympathetic as she spoke. Sarah just nodded, not wanting to talk about it any longer. Sensing her reluctance to speak on the subject, Lydia continued, "How have you been feeling?"

Sarah wanted to cry about just how miserable she was but knew she couldn't, not with everyone around. Instead, she answered, "I have been getting along well enough. I suppose I just find it difficult trying to return to my normal way of things."

"Of course, considering what you have experienced," she returned, then more quietly as she leaned toward Sarah, "And I am sure it must be uncomfortable to be back in the company of people of this sort."

"You know not how I loathe it," Sarah muttered.

"Retribution awaits all liars," she snidely remarked. Sensing the mass would soon begin as Reverend Barnard walked toward the pulpit, Lydia bade Sarah farewell. "I suppose I must go now, I am sitting with my mother today." She gave Sarah's arm a gentle squeeze. "I shall speak to you again soon. And you know I will be here if you need anything."

"Thank you." Sarah smiled at her as she walked away. Part of her wanted Lydia to stay but she knew the younger woman's mother wouldn't allow it.

During the mass, Sarah's mind was not focusing on Barnard's sermon. Instead, frantic thoughts filled her head. She kept having the urge to run away, to just be away from everyone, to be by herself. She felt her resolve breaking and her face twisted as she tried to stop herself from crying. Finally, as people began to get up for communion, she found her opportunity and ran out of the meetinghouse. Her rushing feet brought her to a large rock near the road. She slumped down on it and the tears poured out of her in waves.

Her mind went to thoughts of what people might be saying about her running out of Sabbath meeting. Perhaps they thought she had gone mad and was incapable of conducting herself appropriately in public. Or maybe they believed she really was a witch who could not bear to listen to sermons or prayers. Of course they wouldn't understand. And how could she explain it to people who didn't know what she was experiencing? It was hard enough for her own family to understand it, let alone outsiders. The sound of snow crunching pulled her from her thoughts and she was startled to see Samuel coming toward her. Fiercely, she wiped at her tears to try to hide her current state.

"Sarah, what is wrong?" he asked quietly as he approached her. The question only brought more tears to her eyes and she was unable to answer him. She only shook her head and looked down. He gently laid a hand on her arm and urged her, "Please tell me what troubles you. I mean only to help."

"I… I… do not know," she choked out. "I just had to get away. I always feel like this now. I cannot understand it. I am always sad."

"Well, after what you have been through, how could you expect to feel anything else?" He looked at her with empathic eyes.

"But this… this is different. It… it feels like I am never going to be happy again. I find joy in nothing, not even things I used to love doing." She sobbed more. "I am sorry. I should not be unburdening myself to you like this, especially when I have not seen you since the summer."

"Please, I care for you. I want you to be open with me about how you feel," he urged her softly.

She was about to reply when she saw her brothers heading toward her. "Sarah, what happened?" John asked upon seeing her reddened eyes.

"I just needed to be by myself, I could not stay in there anymore," she said softly. "I am sorry, I… I just could not."

"Well, we are going home now, you can rest in your room if you wish," he replied. He was trying much harder to be sympathetic to her despondent mood.

She nodded before turning to Samuel. "I should go." She tried to give him a reassuring look. "Thank you for your concern."

"Always, but Sarah, I would like to speak with you more, as I have not gotten to in so long," he said pleadingly.

Sarah was unsure how to respond, but Joseph did so for her. "Why not come to our house tomorrow?"

Sarah just glared at her brother, but he pretended not to notice. Samuel, however, noticed Sarah's dismay and asked her, "May I?"

Not wanting to be rude, she nodded. "Yes."

"I will see you tomorrow then." He gave her a small smile, which she tried in vain to return.

As she walked away with her family, she hissed at Joseph, "What did you do that for?"

"I think you have kept the poor man waiting long enough." He shrugged his shoulders. "You cannot hide from him forever."

She grumbled under her breath and walked faster, outpacing her family. Now she had to compose herself in order to talk to Samuel tomorrow. She had been anxious enough just thinking about seeing him again and now her brother was forcing her to confront him.

As the sun rose the next day, Sarah tried desperately to keep herself together. She felt sick and dreaded seeing Samuel. When he finally came, Joseph escorted him inside and, after offering him some refreshment, left him and Sarah alone by the hearth. There was an awkward silence for a moment, with neither knowing how to proceed.

"Sit, please." Sarah gestured at one of the chairs.

He did so and she sat opposite him. "So are… are you feeling any better from yesterday?" he asked.

"Truthfully? No, not at all." She could already hear her voice cracking as she answered. Quickly she changed the subject. "How is your arm?"

"It is much better now," he said, touching where the wound was.

"Good." She nodded.

"Sarah, I would rather hear about you. Your brothers told me you had been sick for weeks, and I hate to say it, but you look as if you are still not completely healthy now." He looked at her earnestly.

"I fear it is now my mind that keeps me from health." She shook her head. "I have been in a constant state of melancholy ever since my mother's death. I thought it would improve once I left prison, but it has only gotten worse."

"How so?" he inquired.

"I constantly have these negative thoughts now. As soon as I wake in the morning, I feel a terrible despair, this ever-present sadness within my body, and I am set to weeping again," she explained. "I keep reliving everything that happened to me and I feel so hopeless. You must think I am crazed."

"No, not at all," he replied. "I think you just need a lot of rest and comfort following what happened to you, and I would like to offer you any help I can give."

"Why would you want to help me? I am not worth it. Why would you even still want me, Sam? Trust me, you do not. You do not want a wife who just lies in bed all day and cries." She hung her head as she started to cry. "I am so broken."

"No, you are not." His voice was soft, barely above a whisper. "Hurt, yes, but not broken." He paused for a brief moment as he took her hand. "When I was told of what befell you and your family, I was in utter disbelief. I cannot begin to comprehend what you went through, what you are still going through, but you are not broken. You just need time to heal, time to collect the pieces of your life and set yourself back onto the right path."

"But how?" she asked. "Nothing brings me any happiness or peace. I find myself crumbling into a dark abyss and I cannot pull myself out of it. I hate feeling this way, but I cannot help it. I find there is no hope for the future. I cannot even find any reason worth living save out of obligation to my family."

Silence fell between them again for a moment before he murmured, "I wish I could take your pain away. But you must find something to live for, something to give you strength," he said as his thumb brushed the back of her hand. "Honestly, I think I can understand how you feel. When I was in Maine, we were ordered to lay waste to the enemies' property, and those people cried for us, begged us to not destroy their homes. I doubt if any of them were deserving of it. I hated having to do that, and those memories still haunt me. When I returned home, I felt so utterly lost, but then I thought of you. You gave me strength when I had none. I thought, if you can survive with all that you have been through, then so can I."

"You hold me in too high regard," she muttered.

"And I think you do not consider yourself highly enough." He smiled at her.

"Yes, well, my mind does not let me think so much of myself anymore," she sighed.

"Sarah, let me tell you something and always remember this: you control your mind, your mind does not control you," he said sternly. "It is a hard battle to fight, but it is a battle you must win."

"Will you stay by my side while I fight it?" she asked tiredly, but with a hint of a smile on her face.

"Every step of the way," he promised. They smiled at each other.

"So we can be broken together then?" She laughed a little at the absurdity of it all.

"Let us try for sanity first." He laughed too, relieved to see her smile.

"If you insist," she said playfully.

"So is it all right if I ask your brothers if I may formally court you?" he asked.

"Yes, by all means," she replied. "I just hope you know what you are getting into with me."

"I suppose I will just have to find out." He gave the back of her hand a quick kiss before bidding her farewell. He found John and Joseph in the kitchen, sharing a drink.

"Well, Samuel, how did it go?" John asked.

"She seems to be in better spirits than yesterday," he replied. "I hope I was able to make her feel better."

"We all hope so as well."

Sam played with his hat for a moment before asking what he really wanted to. "John, Joseph, I would like your permission to court her."

The brothers looked at each other and nodded. They had already agreed to allow Samuel to court their sister. Not only did they like the man immensely, but he had a gentle temperament that would be to Sarah's benefit given everything that she had been through. They also wanted to respect their mother's wishes. Before she died, she had told them to allow the pair to marry if Samuel asked for Sarah's hand.

"You may have it, on one condition," John said as he rose. "You will never hurt her."

"No, of course not," Sam said.

John wrapped an arm around his shoulder and led him over to the window. "Good, because you see that tree out there?" he said, pointing to the yard and watched as the other man nodded. "That is where we buried our mother." He saw Samuel's eyes widen. "And if you ever hurt my sister, you will be buried right beside her. Do I make myself clear?"

"Yes…yes, sir," Sam stuttered.

"Very well then, you may court her." John was amused at how he managed to frighten someone taller and arguably stronger than himself.

"Th… thank you. I shall be taking my leave now, good day," Samuel said abruptly before leaving.

John turned to Joseph. "So do you think I scared him enough?"

Joseph shook his head. "No, he didn't piss himself."

John shrugged. "Next time then."

"So if he asks to marry her, will you say yes?" Joseph asked.

"He can marry her tomorrow if it gets her to stop crying for all I care."

ᦉ

As the months passed, Sarah found herself slowly getting better. With the support of her family and Sam, she found ways to cope with her grief better. It involved a lot of forcing herself to think more positively about situations and pushing the negative thoughts away. She also thought a lot about the things she had to be grateful for in her life. She took walks often and spent a lot of time outdoors once the weather got warmer, which helped improve her mood as well. The road back to happiness was difficult to navigate, but she managed to walk it, with a few stumbles here and there.

Things had also changed in the Parker household. Ann had her baby in June, another boy they named Benjamin. Jacob finally got his first pair of breeches

on his fifth birthday and wore them proudly. Then
there were the changes in sleeping arrangements. The
siblings decided to give Peter Mary's old room and
Joseph would be getting Sarah's because she too
would finally be leaving them. Samuel asked to marry
her and had gotten John's blessing. Sam suggested
they have their wedding in September, his idea of
turning her focus away from the anniversary of her
mother's death. Sarah agreed, thinking perhaps
replacing a bad memory with a good one would be
best. Ann convinced Sarah to make a new dress after
burning her black one and Sarah wanted to have it
ready in time for her wedding. Together Ann and
Sarah went to a local merchant to look at the fabrics
he had available. She chose a rich forest green wool
for the dress and embroidered the neckline and cuffs
with red and pink roses. The roses were inspired by
the ones she grew in the garden. They came back
healthier and more vibrant this year much to her
satisfaction.

The night before her wedding, she went out to
the great oak. She laid down the remaining roses from
the garden on top of her mother's grave. Grass had
started to cover the dirt plot and would hide it
eventually. Had the burial not been illegal, they would
have erected a gravestone. Since that was not an
option, Sarah would just have to commit the gravesite
to memory.

"Tomorrow I will be wed," she spoke to her
mother. "At least you and I no longer have to fear
that not happening." She sighed. "I wish you could be
here for it… though I have a feeling you will be. You

have always been watching over me, haven't you? All those times I thought I saw or heard you in the house, I knew... I just knew you were still with me, like you said you would be. I just hope I have not disappointed you too much."

For a time she said nothing, almost as if hoping her mother would speak back to her. But all she heard was the gentle rustle of leaves as a soft breeze blew. She smiled sadly. "I miss you so much. I think of you every day." She looked up at the sky as dusk approached and the moon hung overhead. "Tomorrow begins a new part of my life. Wish me luck," she said, then whispered, "I love you, Mama."

She looked back toward the moon. She had made peace with the earth's satellite since her time in prison. The comfort it brought her returned once again. As she thought back on it now, it was good that the moon was always there in the sky, the one constant that was present in her chaotic life. She gave it a genuine smile as she took in the silent understanding that she would always have a friend called the moon for as long as she lived.

The next morning she was in her room getting dressed. Her linens had all been washed and were now fresh and clean for her special day. She took a moment to admire the green fabric of her new dress as it shone brightly in the sunlight that filtered in through the window. She looked at the embroidered roses and decided that she was pleased with her stitch work. She had just finished dressing when there was a knock at the door.

"Come in!" she called.

"The dress came out beautifully." John smiled at her as he entered her room with a small package in his hand.

"Thank you." She returned his smile.

"Nervous?" he asked.

"Surprisingly, no," she said thoughtfully. "You would think I would be, but I suppose after everything else I went through, this should be of no trouble at all."

"Good. I have something for you." He raised the package. "We found it when we went through Mother's things. I think she meant to give it to you on your wedding day, so here it is."

"What is it?" she asked as she took the package.

"I suppose you will have to open it to find out. I will leave you to it," he smirked and walked out of the room.

Sarah sat on the bed and slowly untied the strings of the package. Unfolding the paper, she found a pristine white linen fabric inside of it. Slowly unfolding the fabric, she realized it was an apron. On the lower right corner, her mother had embroidered two large roses, one red and one pink. Near the roses, she embroidered two fireflies in flight. So this was what her mother had been making before she died. It was Mary's custom. She had made Hannah and Elizabeth embroidered aprons prior to their weddings as well.

"Oh, Mother," Sarah whispered sadly as she ran her fingers over the satin stitches. "Trying to make me cry on my wedding day, are you?" She sniffled tightly. "No, I promised myself that this is one day I will not cry."

With great pride, she stood and tied the apron around her waist. It was the perfect complement to her rose-embroidered dress. In this way, she could at least have her mother present for her marriage. When she had finished readying herself for the day, she descended the stairs and found all of her family members gathered in the main room, including her cousins and Aunt Mary.

They all turned when Ann spoke. "Oh, Sarah, you look so beautiful! Such wonderful work you did on that dress."

"Thank you." She smiled at Ann.

"Oh, Sarah, if only your mother could see you," Aunt Mary said. She got teary-eyed as she looked at her niece.

"She sees, trust me," Sarah said reassuringly.

Then Aunt Mary suddenly became hysterical and started to wail out, "It's not fair! It's not fair what they did to her!"

They were all taken aback by her outburst. "Mother, please, not now," Stephen pleaded with her.

"I cannot help it. They did wrong to all of us," she cried.

"Mother, this is not the time for this," he reprimanded her.

"You do not understand. None of you do!"

Stephen was about to interject again, but Sarah stopped him. She gently took her aunt's hands. "I understand," she said calmly.

"You do?" Aunt Mary sniffled as she looked up at Sarah.

"Yes, I understand," she said seriously. "I understand that this world eats away at you, takes you apart piece by piece until it feels like there is nothing left. And when they have done all that they can to ruin you, society does nothing to help you. But we cannot let them take away that inner light, that last shred of hope that we have deep inside of us. They do not deserve it. It belongs to you and only you."

Mary's face relaxed and she breathed, "Thank you. I will not let them take my light."

Sarah wrapped her aunt in a firm hug to let her know she wasn't alone. She spoke as she pulled away. "Now, I want you to stop crying because today is to be a joyous day. I want no tears save from happiness on my wedding day. Is that understood?"

"Yes, perfectly." Aunt Mary smiled at her then.

The rest of the day followed as a celebration. After the marriage ceremony, there was good food to be had and much merriment. And for once, Sarah was looking forward to the future.

EPILOGUE

It has been ten years since those events. Ten years on and I know I will never completely recover. I bear scars that will never fade. Some are visible, like the one on my wrist, others are unseen and those are the ones that hurt the most. So much has changed in my life, and yet the past never really dies for me.

I have lost more people along the way, including Sam's father who died of illness. And I never saw Martha again after I was released from prison, but I think of her from time to time. I heard a rumor once about a widower who married his indentured servant once her debt had been paid. I laugh every time I think it may have been Martha. Of course, she would be the type to get a husband out of those circumstances. Wherever she is, I wish her the best and hope that she has found some peace. I try not to get too attached to people outside of my family anymore, because I know one day I will have to lose them.

After a long day of working in the fields, I tuck my boys into bed. "Mama, will the baby be a boy or a girl?" my youngest, Richard, asks, alluding to my swollen belly. We named him after Sam's father, who died only months before he was born.

"We will have to wait until the babe is born to know," I respond just as I see little Mary waiting for me by the doorway. "Though I believe we may finally get to give your sister a girl to play with."

"Eh, girls are useless," my other boy, Sam, Jr., grumbles.

"Well, without us girls, you would not be here," Mary snaps at him as she folds her arms across her chest. Oh yes, she is definitely my daughter.

"She is right," I say to him in mock sternness. "So you better show us some respect."

"Well, I respect you, Mama. You are a woman," he replies.

"Oh, is that how it is?" They certainly make me laugh. "Goodnight, my little ones." I give each of them a kiss on their forehead as they say goodnight in return. Then I follow Mary to her room and she climbs into bed. "There is no moon tonight," she says sadly.

"No, for a storm is coming," I reply. "It will be out tomorrow night. Would you like to stargaze with me then?"

"Yes, very much!" She smiles brightly.

"Very well, we shall." I kiss her forehead. "Goodnight, my dear."

"Goodnight, Mama," she replies before turning on her side to sleep.

I close the door behind me and return to my own bedroom. Night has fallen and clouds block out the stars as a thunderstorm begins. I close the open window as a light rain begins to hit against the glass. Perhaps I am strange, but I have always found thunderstorms soothing. But then again, I have always been a child of nature, even in its all-powerful and terrifying wrath, for nature has never hurt me. A strike of lightning flashes in the sky and is followed by a powerful thunderclap.

Sam jerks awake, startled by the noise. He is a light sleeper; a habit learned from his time serving with the militia. I sit on the edge of the bed and run my fingers through his hair to soothe him. He is still as handsome as he was when we first married, though his face has matured and lost its boyish features.

"Scared the hell out of me…" he mumbles softly, a small smile gracing his lips. "Are you going to sleep?"

"Yes, my love." My voice contains all the tenderness that my heart can provide.

He nods before he closes his eyes, returning to the fantasy land of whatever dreams he may have. I think back on all the times I must have driven him mad throughout our marriage. There were times when I fell back into that horrible melancholic state. How many times did he hold me as I cried or talk with me late into the night when I could not sleep? But true to his word, he always stayed by my side.

In the corner of the room, I see a small flicker of light. A firefly sits on the wall and every few seconds it flashes its light into the room. "Mother," I whisper, "Are you paying me a visit?" I let the small beetle crawl on my finger before it flies into another corner of the room. I used to think her ghost dwelled within my old home. My brothers tried to convince me that it was only my grief playing tricks on my mind. Perhaps they were right all along, but still, I find it more comforting to believe that she comes to visit every now and then.

Memories of my mother haunt me often. I try to think of the better times though and force my mind not to drift back to that last horrible month of her life. I wish terribly that she was still here. She would have loved her grandchildren. One day I will tell them the truth of their grandmother's fate and take them to visit her gravesite.

Reverend Hale, God rest his soul, once told me that in time, I would see the reason for the horror I and the others endured. In ten years, I have still not found that reason. I suppose I can say that in some ways, it made me a stronger person, but stronger to what end? What exactly was that hardship preparing me for? The sad truth I find is that there is no reason. There is no greater purpose. We must simply accept that terrible things happen to people who are undeserving of it. The more you try to find a justification for the things that happen to you, the more you will drive yourself to insanity.

It is easy to succumb to the darkness, but I have a promise to keep; a promise I made to my mother. Every summer I walk among the fireflies and I feel hope once again. I walk through the fields with my children and catch the small beetles with them. I find my childlike wonder in their awestruck faces, in my husband's arms, and in the blossoms of the flowers that grow every spring. I look at the moon and am amazed by how brightly it shines. I see magnificent power in the rippling waves of the rivers. I see beauty in the changing colors of leaves in autumn.

Everywhere I turn I see life's little miracles and I find peace in them.

I try to find happiness in all of these little things, even when the misery of my past comes back to taunt me. I have accepted that part of my life. It is what made me the person I am today and I carry those memories like battle scars. I wear them with honor. So every now and then, when that shadow that haunts my mind comes back again, I find a vague comfort in it; like I would not know how to live without it. It is a part of me and I am a part of it.

And in the darkness of the night, I feel resolved to affirm to myself, "But I will *never* let you break me."

HISTORICAL NOTES

First, let me begin by stating that I have been interested in the subject of the Salem Witch Trials since I was a child. When I was twelve, I was inspired to write my own story regarding them. I initially had the idea to write about a young woman, around the age of eighteen, whose parent was executed. After some research, I came across Mary Parker of Andover who had a daughter named Sarah, age twenty-two. I also found the Parker family to be good subjects because they were relatively obscure among the victims of the trials and I wanted to tell their story. The original version of this story I wrote as a teenager is much different from the story you have just read, but here are some historical facts that pertain to the story.

The Parker family was one of the founding families of Andover, Massachusetts, with Nathan Parker and his brother Joseph moving there from Newbury, Massachusetts, in the late 1640s to the early 1650s. Nathan Parker was at least ten years older than his wife, Mary Ayer, but I was unable to find birth records for either. Nathan's age is given as about forty-two in 1661 and then about forty in 1662 in the Essex County Court Records, placing his year of birth between 1619 and 1622. Sources typically give Mary's birth year as 1637, but she may have been born a few years earlier. Prior to his marriage with Mary, Nathan had previously been married to Susanna Short, who died in 1651. He appears to have had a son named Nathan, Jr. with her who lived out his life in his father's original town of Newbury. He predeceased his father in 1679. It is uncertain what relationship Nathan, Jr. had with his stepmother and stepsiblings, if he had one with them at all, hence why he is not mentioned in the story. Nathan, Sr. died in 1685, leaving his family with plenty of wealth and property. He and Mary had at least nine children (possibly ten as per Andover's Vital Records) with three having died prior to 1692: James, Mary Jr., and Robert. James was killed along with one of his cousins in battle at Black Point, Maine, in 1677 when members of the Sokosis and Ammoscoggins tribes made a surprise attack on the English.

Mary Parker was brought to Salem for charges of witchcraft in September of 1692. The surviving court records for Mary Ayer Parker in 1692 are few with only her examination, three indictments, and two short pieces of testimony surviving. Outside of her actual court case are the petitions from her sons John and Joseph, one of which is in regards to their seized property. Therefore, in order to recreate what Mary's trial would have looked like, I had to piece together her records with what seems to have occurred at others' trials. She appears to have had her trial by

September 16th and was executed on September 22nd along with seven others. Of the three indictments against her, only the one for afflicting Martha Sprague was returned ignoramus by the grand jury, although the surviving records would lead one to believe this indictment had the most evidence backing it up. No reason is given for the grand jury dropping this charge. A possible reason I gave in the story, and one that I thought would make sense, was that Martha Sprague was simply not there to give testimony. Regardless, the trial jury found enough evidence for the other two indictments to convict Mary. While the location of Mary's grave is unknown, local tradition holds that the relatives of the executed came to retrieve their bodies after nightfall. Thus, this possibility is included in the plot of the story.

The Salem trials mark the first time that Mary Parker appears to have gotten into legal trouble in her life. Jacqueline Kelly, in her essay "The Untold Story of Mary Ayer Parker: Gossip and Confusion in 1692" speculates that a rift between the Parker and Chandler families may have been behind her accusation. This is largely based on the apprenticeship dispute between the Tylers and Chandlers. In 1662, Thomas Chandler brought suit against Job Tyler for his son Moses breaking his younger brother Hopestill's apprenticeship contract and helping Hopestill to run away from Chandler. A few years before, the two families had asked Nathan Parker to write up the apprenticeship contract and keep it in his possession. When Nathan and Mary were not home, Moses along with accomplice John Godfrey stole and burned the contract. Nathan testified to this in court and Chandler won the suit and Hopestill had to go back to Chandler. In her essay, Kelly wonders if the Chandlers thought the Parkers favored the Tylers, especially when their children Hannah Parker and John Tyler later married. However, Nathan's testimony during the apprenticeship dispute was damaging for the Tylers and in fact, if anyone, it would have been the Tylers who resented the Parkers after the fact. It also does not consider the fact that during the Salem trials, several members of the Tyler family, even more than those mentioned in the story, were accused, with one of their own, Martha Sprague, aiding in the accusations. Martha Sprague, who was the stepdaughter of Moses Tyler, accused some of her own stepfamily members. Author Richard Hite claims that it is possible Martha Sprague accused Mary Parker because of mentions Moses Tyler may have made about the apprenticeship dispute decades earlier.

Kelly also discusses the possibility that Mary Parker may have been mistaken for her sister-in-law, whose name was also Mary Parker. This Mary Parker, the widow of Nathan's brother Joseph, appears to have suffered from some sort of mental instability. Her son Stephen petitioned the Salem Quarterly Court in 1685 "…that his mother 'is in a distracted condition, and not capable of improving any of her estate for her own comfort & also having some money come from England … to request this Honored Court to empower myself or some other, to receive said money (being about ten pounds)…'" It is unclear what this Mary's mental condition was but it could possibly have caused misgivings about her character in the community. Kelly postulates that she was confused with her sister-in-law in 1692, leading to

Mary Ayer Parker's death. Regardless, I chose to include this Mary's condition in the story as it fit into the novel's theme of mental illness.

There are even fewer records concerning Mary Ayer Parker's daughter Sarah, who was also accused of witchcraft in 1692. In fact, there are no court records that survive in regards to Sarah's case itself from that year. The only time her name is brought up in 1692 is when three other women, Elizabeth Johnson, Sr., Rebecca Eames, and Susannah Post, mention her in their own examinations, with what they said about her included in Sarah's examination scene in the story. Therefore, we cannot know with certainty what may have been said by either Sarah herself or the afflicted at her examination, if she even had one. This also leads us to question whether she confessed like so many others in Andover or if she followed in her mother's footsteps and maintained her innocence. However, Sarah herself does give us a vital piece of information in her request for restitution in 1712. She states that she was in Salem prison for seventeen weeks in 1692. As the examinations of the three women who mentioned her occurred from August 19th to 30th in 1692, we can assume that Sarah was imprisoned at the same time if not slightly before her mother. Seventeen weeks from then would place her release from prison near the end of December. In the story, I chose to postpone her imprisonment until after her mother's execution. Although in real life, it is interesting to note that if Sarah was formally accused before her mother, the suspicion of witchcraft on her may have spurred suspicion of her mother. Also, if Sarah was indeed released from prison in December, no court proceedings were occurring at this time, so I assume she was released through a note of recognizance, a form of bail. Other families were doing the same for their loved ones at this time as well. Furthermore, there is no record of a trial for her when the court reconvened in 1693, so her case was most likely dismissed.

Sadly, Sarah largely disappears from the records after 1692. There is no marriage or death record for her. In her previously mentioned letter to the court in 1712, she signs only with the name of Parker. This most certainly means she never married, although author Hite mentions the slim possibility that she may have married a man who also bore the last name of Parker. Although I do not know for certain what her fate was, I felt she deserved a happier ending in the story.

That being said, the characters of Samuel Galler and his family, Martha Upton, and Lydia Holten never existed and are my own creations. The names of some characters were also changed to prevent confusion. The name of John Parker's eldest son was changed to Jacob from John and Hannah's and Elizabeth's husbands' names were also changed to Daniel and Henry, respectively, from John. Likewise, Ann Parker's name was also changed from Hannah to prevent confusion with the Parkers' sister. As a side note, in 1683 Hannah Parker's husband, John Tyler, confessed to fornication with her prior to their marriage. He was sentenced to either pay a fine or be whipped and she had to pay a fine. Interestingly, despite this previous history and having members of both her birth family and married family embroiled in the witch hunt, Hannah Parker herself managed to avoid suspicion of witchcraft in 1692.

Outside of the Parker family's history, I tried to remain true to the historical facts of the Salem Witch Trials and the time period in general. Some of the lesser characters that appear in the story like Reverends Dane and Barnard, Magistrates Stoughton and Hathorne, and the witnesses against Mary and Sarah were indeed historical figures. In particular, I included Reverend John Hale, as I have always found him an interesting figure and his background information in the story is true to history. Much of his thoughts regarding the trials I tried to glean from his own book, *A Modest Inquiry into the Nature of Witchcraft*. The conditions in Salem jail were accurate based on the sources I could find and Martha's character represents the diversity of the prison population as others besides accused witches would be imprisoned. Although, it should be noted that fornication would generally be punished with a fine or whipping only, but I embellished a bit. Martha's case also shows how some prisoners, regardless of the crime, would have to resort to indenturing themselves if they could not pay their jail fees any other way.

Outside of the witchcraft accusations, the colonists of New England were living against the backdrop of King William's War in 1692. The fear of raids undoubtedly caused more paranoia within their communities. Governor William Phips along with militiamen from several counties went to build Fort William Henry at Pemaquid, Maine, in the summer of 1692. He gave Major Benjamin Church orders to destroy French and Native American enemies and their sustenance at his discretion and to bring back any captives. The extent to which these orders were carried out is largely exaggerated through Samuel's experiences in the story, which I did to emphasize the constant turmoil the English colonists had with their enemies in the northeast.

As to mental illness, the Puritans ascribed the causes of it to physical and/or spiritual ailments. They believed "madness" could be caused by such things as physical injury or disease, demonic possession, a weakness in reason or temperament, or punishment for sinful behavior. Their cures for mental health issues could be spiritual in nature, with fasting and prayer and repentance commonly prescribed remedies, or physical in design including cures like industrious labor, purgatives, bloodletting, herbal mixtures, and other concoctions that are outright bizarre by today's standards. It may surprise some that 17th century Puritans were much more tolerant and supportive of the mentally ill than later generations. They created laws to ensure that communities were providing for the mentally ill when they could neither care for themselves nor had family that could sufficiently do so for them.

BIBLIOGRAPHY

Baxter, Richard. "The Cure of Melancholy and Overmuch Sorrow, by Faith and Physic." *The Practical Works of the Rev. Richard Baxter*, Mills, Jowett, and Mills, 1830, pp. 236-285.

Boyer, Paul, and Stephen Nissenbaum, editors. *The Salem Witchcraft Papers*. Da Capo Press, 1977.

Dow, George Francis, editor. *Records and Files of the Quarterly Courts of Essex County*. Essex Institute, 1911-1975.

Eldridge, Larry D. "'Crazy Brained': Mental Illness in Colonial America." *Bulletin of the History of Medicine*, vol. 70, no. 3, 1996, pp. 361-386.

Hale, John. *A Modest Enquiry into the Nature of Witchcraft*. Boston, 1702. Applewood Books, 1973.

Hite, Richard. *In the Shadow of Salem: The Andover Witch Hunt of 1692*. Westholme Publishing, 2018.

Kelly, Jacqueline. "The Untold Story of Mary Ayer Parker: Gossip and Confusion in 1692." University of Virginia: Salem Witch Trials Documentary Archive and Transcription Project, June 2005, http://salem.lib.virginia.edu/people/?group.num=all.

Norton, Mary Beth. *In the Devil's Snare: The Salem Witchcraft Crisis of 1692*. Alfred A. Knopf of Random House, Inc., 2002.

Roach, Marilynne K. *The Salem Witch Trials: A Day-by-Day Chronicle of a Community Under Siege*. Taylor Trade Publishing, 2004.

Tannenbaum, Rebecca. *Health and Wellness in Colonia America*. Greenwood of ABC-CLIO, LLC., 2012.

Vital Records of Andover Massachusetts. 1912. Cornell University Library, 2007.

ACKNOWLEDGMENTS

When I wrote the first version of this story at the age of twelve, I never imagined that I would actually be publishing it over ten years later. This book probably would not have been published without my parents, Darlene and Bill, who encouraged me throughout this entire process and listened as I went on and on about all of the information I had researched. I would also like to thank my other family members and friends for supporting me through this journey, especially Cynthia Youngclaus, who was my beta reader.

First, I would like to thank Christine LePorte for editing my manuscript and giving me helpful notes. I would also like to thank Rachel Christ, Director of Education at the Salem Witch Museum, for answering my various questions and suggesting research materials to me. Likewise, thanks to Hannah Swan, Reference Assistant at the Phillips Library, Peabody Essex Museum, for conducting research for me. Special thanks to Melissa Macfie, author of *The Celtic Prophecy* series, who answered all of my questions concerning publishing. And last, but not least, thank you to the internet and all of the universities and organizations who make records, research documents, and so much more information easily accessible.